forever free

Ace Science Fiction Books by
Joe Haldeman

WORLDS APART
DEALING IN FUTURES
FOREVER PEACE
FOREVER FREE

Ace Science Fiction Books Edited by
Joe Haldeman

BODY ARMOR: 2000
NEBULA AWARD STORIES SEVENTEEN
SUPERTANKS
SPACEFIGHTERS

Ace Science Fiction Books by
Joe Haldeman and Jack C. Haldeman, II

THERE IS NO DARKNESS

forever free

JOE HALDEMAN

ACE BOOKS, NEW YORK

FOREVER FREE

An Ace Book
Published by The Berkley Publishing Group,
a division of Penguin Putnam Inc.,
375 Hudson Street, New York, New York 10014.
The Penguin Putnam Inc. World Wide Web site address is
http://www.penguinputnam.com

First edition: December 1999

Library of Congress Cataloging-in-Publication Data

Haldeman, Joe W.
        Forever free / by Joe Haldeman.
            p.   cm.
        ISBN 0-441-00697-3
        I. Title.
        PS3558.A353F59   1999
        813'.54—dc21   99-33231
                                                        CIP

Printed in the United States of America

                10   9   8   7   6   5   4   3   2   1

Men stop war to make gods
sometimes. Peace gods, who would make
Earth a haven. A place for men to
think and love and play. No war
to cloud their minds and hearts. Stop,
somehow, men from being men.

Gods make war to stop men
from becoming gods.
Without the beat of drums to stop
our ears, what heaven we could make
of Earth! The anchor that is war
left behind? Somehow free to

stop war? Gods make men to
be somewhat like them. So men
express their godliness in war.
To take life: this is what gods
do. Not the womanly urge to make
life. Nor the simple sense to stop.

War-men make gods. To stop
those gods from raging, we have to
find the heart and head to make
new gods, who don't take men
in human sacrifice. New gods,
who find disgust in war.

Gods stop, to make men war
for their amusement. We can stop
their fun. We can make new gods
in human guise. No need to
call to heaven. Just take plain men
and show to them the heaven they could make!

To stop God's wars! Men make
their own destiny. We don't need war
to prove to anyone that we are men.
But even that is not enough. To stop
war, we have to become more. To
stop war, we have to become gods.

　　　　To stop war, make men gods.

For Gay, again,
twenty-five years later.

forever free

book one

THE BOOK OF GENESIS

Winter is a long time coming on this god-forsaken planet, and it stays too long, too. I watched a sudden gust blow a line of cold foam across the grey lake and thought about Earth, not for the first time that day. The two warm winters in San Diego when I was a boy. Even the bad winters in Nebraska. They were at least short.

Maybe we were too quick to say no, when the magnanimous zombies offered to share Earth with us, after the war. We didn't really get rid of them, coming here.

Cold radiated from the windowpane. Marygay cleared her throat behind me. "What is it?" she said.

"Looks like weather. I ought to check the trotlines."

"Kids will be home in an hour."

"Better I do it now, dry, than all of us stand out in the rain," I said. "Snow, whatever."

"Probably snow." She hesitated, and didn't offer to help. After twenty years she could tell when I didn't want company. I pulled on wool sweater and cap and left the rain slicker on its peg.

I stepped out into the damp hard wind. It didn't smell like snow coming. I asked my watch and it said 90 percent rain, but a cold front in the evening would bring freezing rain and snow. That would make for a fun meeting. We had to walk a couple of klicks, there and back. Otherwise the zombies could look through transportation records and see that all of us paranoids had converged on one house.

We had eight trotlines that stretched out ten meters from the end of the dock to posts I'd sunk in the chest-deep water. Two more had been knocked down in a storm; I'd replace them come spring. Two years from now, in real years.

It was more like harvesting than fishing. The blackfish are so dumb they'll bite anything, and when they're hooked and thrash around, it attracts other blackfish: "Wonder what's wrong with that guy—oh, look! Somebody's head on a nice shiny hook!"

When I got out on the dock I could see thunderheads building in the east, so I worked pretty fast. Each trotline's a pulley that supports a dozen hooked leaders dangling in the water, held to one-meter depth with plastic floaters. It looked like half the floaters were down, maybe fifty fish. I did a mental calculation and realized I'd probably just finish the last one when Bill got home from school. But the storm was definitely coming.

I took work gloves and apron off a hook by the sink and hauled the end of the first line up to the eye-level pulley wheel. I opened the built-in freezer—the stasis field inside reflected the angry sky like a pool of mercury—and wheeled in the first fish.

Worked it off the hook, chopped off the head and tail with a cleaver, threw the fish into the freezer, and then rebaited the hook with its head. Then rolled in the next client.

Three of the fish were the useless mutant strain we've been getting for more than a year. They're streaked with pink and have a noxious hydrogen-sulfide taste. The blackfish won't take them for bait and I can't even use them for fertilizer; you might as well scatter your soil with salt.

Maybe an hour a day—half that, with the kids helping—and we supplied about a third of the fish for the village. I didn't eat much of it myself. We also bartered corn, beans, and asparagus, in their seasons.

Bill got off the bus while I was working on the last line. I waved him inside; no need for both of us to get all covered with fish guts and blood. Then lightning struck on the other side of the lake and I put the line back in anyhow. Hung up the stiff gloves and apron and turned off the stasis field for a second to check the catch level.

Just beat the rain. I stood on the porch for a minute and watched the squall line hiss its way across the lake.

Warm inside; Marygay had started a small fire in the kitchen fireplace. Bill was sitting there with a glass of wine. That was still a novelty to him. "So how are we doing?" His accent always sounded strange when he first got back from school. He didn't speak English in class or, I suspected, with many of his friends.

"Over the sixty percent mark," I said, scrubbing my hands and face at the work sink. "Any better luck and we'll have to eat the damned things ourselves."

"Think I'll poach a big bunch for dinner," Marygay said, deadpan. That gave them the flavor and consistency of cotton.

"Come on, Mom," Bill said. "Let's just have them raw." He

liked them even less than I did. Chopping off their heads was the high point of his day.

I went to the trio of casks at the other end of the room and tapped a glass of dry red wine, then sat with Bill on the bench by the fire. I poked at it with a stick, a social gesture probably older than this young planet.

"You were going to have the art zombie today?"

"The art history *Man*," he said. "She's from Centrus. Haven't seen her in a year. We didn't draw or anything; just looked at pictures and statues."

"From Earth?"

"Mostly."

"Tauran art is weird." That was a charitable assessment. It was also ugly and incomprehensible.

"She said we have to come to it gradually. We looked at some architecture."

Their architecture, I knew something about. I'd destroyed acres of it, centuries ago. Felt like yesterday sometimes.

"I remember the first time I came across one of their barracks," I said. "All the little individual cells. Like a beehive."

He made a noncommital noise that I took as a warning. "So where's your sister?" She was still in high school but had the same bus. "I can't keep her schedule straight."

"She's at the library," Marygay said. "She'll call if she's going to be late."

I checked my watch. "Can't wait dinner too long." The meeting was at eight and a half.

"I know." She stepped over the bench and sat down between us, and handed me a plate of breadsticks. "From Snell, came by this morning."

They were salty and hard; broke between the jaws with an interesting concussion. "I'll thank him tonight."

6

"Old folks party?" Bill asked.

"Sixday," I said. "We're walking, if you want the floater."

" 'But don't drink too much wine,' " he anticipated, and held up his glass. "This is it. Volleyball down at the gym."

"Win one for the Gipper."

"What?"

"Something my mother used to say. I don't know what a gipper is."

"Sounds like a position," he said. "Server, spiker, gipper." As if he cared a lot about the game *qua* game. They played in the nude, mixed, and it was as much a mating ritual as a sport.

A sudden blast of sleet rattled against the window. "You don't want to walk through that," he said. "You could drop me off at the gym."

"Well, you could drop *us* off," Marygay said. The route of the floater wasn't registered; just the parking location, supposedly for call forwarding. "Charlie and Diana's place. They won't care if we're early."

"Thanks. I might score." He didn't mean volleyball. When he used our ancient slang I never knew whether it was affection or derision. I guess when I was twenty-one I could do both at the same time, with my parents.

A bus stopped outside. I heard Sara running up the boardwalk through the weather. The front door opened and shut fast, and she ran upstairs to change.

"Dinner in ten minutes," Marygay called up the stairs. She made an impatient noise back.

"Starting to bleed tomorrow," Bill said.

"Since when do brothers keep track of that," Marygay said. "Or husbands?"

He looked at the floor. "She said something this morning."

I broke the silence. "If there are any Men there tonight . . ."

"They never come. But I won't tell them you're off plotting."

"It's not *plotting*," Marygay said. "Planning. We'll tell them eventually. But it's a human thing." We hadn't discussed it with him or Sara, but we hadn't tried to keep them from overhearing.

"I could come someday."

"Someday," I said. Probably not. So far it was all first-generation; all vets, plus their spouses. Only a few of them, spouses, were born on this thing Man had called a "garden planet," when they gave us a choice of places to relocate after the war.

We usually called "our" planet MF. Most of the people who lived here were dozens of generations away from appreciating what we'd meant by "middle finger." Even if they did know, they probably didn't connect the acronym with the primal Oedipal act.

After living through an entire winter, though, they probably called the planet their cultures' versions of "motherfucker."

MF had been presented to us as a haven and a refuge—and a place of reunion. We could carve out an existence here as plain humans, without interference from Man, and if you had friends or lovers lost in the relativistic maze of the Forever War, you could wait for them on the *Time Warp*, a converted battlewagon that shuttled back and forth between Mizar and Alcor fast enough to almost halt aging.

Of course it turned out that Man did want to keep an eye on us, since we comprised a sort of genetic insurance policy.

They could use us as a baseline if, after X generations, something bad cropped up in their carbon-copy genetic pattern. (I once used that term with Bill, and started to explain, but he did know what carbon copies were. Like he knew what cave paintings were.)

But they weren't passive observers. They were zookeepers. And MF did resemble a zoo: an artificial simplified environment. But the zookeepers didn't build it. They just stumbled onto it.

Middle Finger, like all the Vega-class planets we'd found, was an anomaly and a cartoon. It defied normal models of planetary formation and evolution.

A too-young bright blue star with a single planet, Earth-sized with oxygen-water chemistry. The planet orbits at a distance where life can be sustained, if only just.

(Planet people tell us that there's no way to have an Earth-type planet unless you also have a Jupiter-type giant in the system. But then stars like Vega and Mizar shouldn't have Earths anyhow.)

Middle Finger has seasons, but they're provided not by inclination toward the sun, but by the long oval of its orbit. We have six seasons spread over three Earth years: spring, summer, fall, first winter, deep winter, and thaw. Of course the planet moves slower, the farther it is from its sun, so the cold seasons are long, and the warm ones, short.

Most of the planet is arctic waste or dry tundra. Here at the equator, lakes and streams ice over in deep winter. Toward the poles, lakes are solid permanent ice from the surface down, with sterile puddles forming on warm summer days. Two-thirds of the planet's surface is lifeless except for airborne spores and micro-organisms.

The ecology is curiously simple, too—fewer than a hundred

9

native varieties of plants; about the same number of insects and things that resemble arthropods. No native mammals, but a couple of dozen species of large and small things that are roughly reptiles or amphibians. Only seven kinds of fish, and four aquatic mollusks.

Nothing has evolved from anything else. There are no fossils, because there hasn't been enough time—carbon dating says nothing on or near the surface is more than ten thousand years old. But core samples from less than fifty meters down reveal a planet as old as Earth.

It's as if somebody had hauled a planet here and parked it, seeded with simple life. But where did they haul it from, and who are they, and who paid the shipping bill? All of the energy expended by the humans and the Taurans during the Forever War wouldn't have moved this planet far.

It's a mystery to them, too; the Taurans, which I find reassuring.

There are other mysteries that are not reassuring. Chief among them is that this corner of the universe had been inhabited before, up to about five thousand years ago.

The nearest Tauran planet, Tsogot, had been discovered and colonized during the Forever War. They found the ruins of a huge city there, larger than New York or London, buried in drifting dunes. The husks of dozens of alien spaceships drifted in orbit, one of them an interstellar vessel.

Of the creatures who had built this powerful civilization, not a clue. They left behind no statues or pictures, which may be explainable in terms of culture. Neither did they leave any bodies, not even a single bone, which is harder to explain.

The Tauran name for them is Boloor, "the lost."

forever free

*   *   *

usually cooked on Sixday, since I didn't teach then, but the Greytons had brought by a couple of rabbits, and that was Marygay's specialty, hassenpfeffer. The kids liked it better than most Earth food. They mostly preferred the bland native stuff, which is all they got at school. Marygay says it's a natural survival trait; even on Earth, children stuck to bland, familiar food. *I* hadn't, but then my parents were strange, hippies. We ate fiery Indian food. I never tasted meat until I was twelve, when California law made them send me to school.

Dinner was amusing, Bill and Sara trading gossip about their friends' dating and mating. Sara's finally gotten over Taylor, who had been her steady for a year, and Bill had welcome news about a social disaster the boy had caused. It had stung her when he declared himself home, but after a few months' fling he turned het again, and asked her to take him back. She told him to stick to boys. Now it turns out he *did* have a boyfriend over in Hardy, very secret, who got mad at him and came over to the college to make a loud public scene. It involved sexual details that we didn't used to discuss at the dinner table. But times change, and fun is fun.

The thing we were plotting actually grew out of an innocent bantering argument I'd had with Charlie and Diana some months before. Diana had been my medical officer during the Sade-138 campaign, our last, out in the Greater Magellanic Cloud; Charlie had served as my XO. Diana had delivered both Bill and Sara. They were our best friends.

Most of the community had taken Sixday off to get together at the Larsons' for a barn-raising. Teresa was an old vet, two campaigns, but her wife Ami was third-generation Paxton. She was our age, biologically, and they had two fusion-clone teenaged daughters. One was off at university, but the other, Sooz, greeted us warmly and was in charge of the coffee and tea.

The hot drinks were welcome; it was unseasonably cold for late spring. It was also muddy. Middle Finger had weather control that was usually reliable—or used to be—but we'd had too much rain the previous couple of weeks, and moving clouds around didn't seem to help. The rain gods were angry. Or happy, or careless; never could tell about gods.

The first couple to arrive, as usual, were Cat and Aldo Verdeur-Sims. And as usual, Cat and Marygay embraced warmly, but only for an instant, out of consideration for their husbands.

On her last mission Marygay, like me, was a het throwback in a world otherwise 100 percent home. Unlike me, she overcame her background and managed to fall in love with a woman, Cat. They were together for a few months, but during their last battle, Cat was severely wounded and went straight to the hospital planet Heaven.

Marygay assumed that was it; the physics of relativity and collapsar jump would separate them by years or centuries. So she came here to wait for me—not for Cat—on the *Time Warp*. She told me all about Cat soon after we got together, and I didn't think it was a big deal; a reasonable adjustment under the circumstances. I'd always been easier with female homosex than male, anyhow.

So right after Sara was born, who should appear but Cat. She'd met Aldo on Heaven and heard about Middle Finger, and the two of them switched to het—something Man could easily do for you and, at that time, was required if you were going to Middle Finger. She knew Marygay was here, from Stargate records, and the space-time geometry worked out all right. She showed up about ten Earth years younger than Marygay and I were. And beautiful.

We got along well—Aldo and I played chess and go together—but you'd have to be blind not to see the occasional wistfulness that passed between Cat and Marygay. We sometimes kidded one another about it, but there was an edge to the joking. Aldo was more nervous about it than me, I think.

Sara came along with us, and Bill would come with Charlie and Diana after church let out. We unbelievers got to pay for our intellectual freedom by donning work boots and slogging through the mud, pounding in the reference stakes for the pressor field generator.

We borrowed the generator from the township, and along with it got the only Man involved in the barn-raising. She would have come anyway, as building inspector, after we had the thing up.

The generator was worth its weight in bureaucrats, though. It couldn't lift the metal girders; that took a lot of human muscle working together. But once they were in position, it kept them in place and perfectly aligned. Like a petty little god that was annoyed by things that weren't at right angles.

I had gods on the brain. Charlie and Diana had joined this new church, Spiritual Rationalism, and had dragged Bill into it. Actually, they didn't have gods in the old sense, and it all seemed reasonable enough, people trying to put some poetry and numinism into their everyday lives. I think Marygay would have gone along with it, if it weren't for my automatic resistance to religion.

Lar Po had surveying tools, including an ancient laser collimator that wasn't much different from the one I'd used in graduate school. We still had to slog through the mud and pound stakes, but at least we knew the stakes were going where they belonged.

The township also supplied a heavy truck full of fiber mastic, more reliable than cement in this climate, and easier to handle. It stayed liquid until it was exposed to an ultrasonic tone that was two specific frequencies in a silent chord. Then it froze permanently solid. You wanted to make sure you didn't have any on your hands or clothes when they turned on the chime.

The piles of girders and fasteners were a kit that had come in a big floater from Centrus. Paxton was allotted such things on the basis of a mysterious formula involving population and productivity and the phases of the moons. We actually could have had two barns this spring, but only the Larsons wanted one.

By the time we had it staked out, about thirty people had showed up. Teresa had a clipboard with job assignments and a timeline for putting the thing up. People took their assignments good-naturedly from "Sergeant Larson, sir." Actually, she'd been a major, like me.

Charlie and I worked together on the refrigeration unit. We'd learned the hard way the first years on this planet, that any permanent building bigger than a shed had to sit on ice year-round. If you carve down to the permafrost and lay a regular foundation, the long bitter winters crack it. So we just give in to the climate and build on ice, or frozen mud.

It was easy work, but sloppy. Another team nailed together a rectangular frame around what would be the footprint of the building, plus a few centimeters every way. Max Weston, one of the few guys big enough to wrestle with it, used an air hammer to pound alloy rods well below the frost line, every meter or so along the perimeter. These would anchor the barn against the hurricane-force winds that made farming such an interesting gamble here. (The weather-control satellites couldn't muster enough power to deflect them.)

Charlie and I slopped around in the mud, connecting long plastic tubes in a winding snake back and forth in what would be the building's sub-foundation. It was just align-glue-drop; align-glue-drop, until we were both half drunk from the glue fumes. Meanwhile, the crew that had nailed up the frame hosed water into the mud, so it would be nice and deep and soupy when we froze it.

We finished and hooked the loose ends up to a compressor and turned it on. Everybody took a break while we watched the mud turn to slush and harden.

It was warmer inside, but Charlie and I were too bespattered to feel comfortable in anyone's kitchen, so we just sat on a stack of foamsteel girders and let Sooz bring us tea.

I waved at the rectangle of mud. "Pretty complex behavior for a bunch of lab rats."

Charlie was still a little dull from the glue. "We have rats?"

"A breeding herd of lab rats."

Then he nodded and sipped some tea. "You're too pessimistic. We'll outlast them. That's one thing I have faith in."

"Yeah, faith can move mountains. Planets." Charlie didn't deny the obvious: that we were animals in a zoo, or a lab. We were allowed to breed freely on Middle Finger in case something went wrong with the grand experiment that was Man: billions of genetically identical non-individuals sharing a single consciousness. Or billions of test-tube twins sharing a mutual data base, if you wanted to be accurate.

We could clone like them, no law against it, if we wanted a son or daughter identical to us, or fusion-clone like Teresa and Ami, if some biological technicality made normal childbirth impossible.

But the main idea was to keep churning out offspring with a wild mix of genes. Just in case something went wrong with perfection. We were their insurance policy.

People had started coming to Middle Finger as soon as the Forever War was over. Vet immigration, spread out over centuries because of relativity, finally totaled a couple of thousand people, maybe ten percent of the present population. We tended to stick together, in small towns like Paxton. We were used to dealing with each other.

Charlie lit up a stick and offered me one; I declined. "I think we could outlast them," I said, "if they let us survive."

"They need us. Us lab rats."

"No, they just need our gametes. Which they can freeze indefinitely in liquid helium."

"Yeah, I can see that. They line us up for sperm and egg samples and then kill us off. They aren't cruel, William, or stupid, no matter what you think of them."

The Man came out to get the manual for her machine, and took it back to the kitchen. They all looked alike, of course, but with considerable variation as they got older. Handsome, tall, swarthy, black-haired, broad of chin and forehead. This one had lost the little finger of her left hand, and for some reason hadn't had it grow back. Probably not worth the time and pain, come to think of it. A lot of us vets remembered the torture of regrowing limbs and members.

When she was out of earshot, I continued. "They wouldn't kill us off, but they wouldn't have to. Once they had sufficient genetic material, they could round us up and sterilize us. Let the experiment run down, one natural death at a time."

"You're cheerful today."

"I'm just blowin' smoke." Charlie nodded slowly. We didn't have the same set of idioms, born six hundred years apart. "But it could happen, if they saw us as a political threat. They get along fine with the Taurans now, but *we're* the wild card. No group mind to commune with."

"So what would you do, fight them? We're not summer chickens anymore."

"That's 'spring' chickens."

"I know, William. We're not even *summer* chickens."

I clicked my cup against his. "Your point. But we're still young enough to fight."

"With what? Your fishing lines and my tomato stakes?"

"They're not heavily armed, either." But as I said that, I felt a sudden chill. As Charlie enumerated the weapons we did know them to have, it occurred to me that we were in a critical historical period, the last time in human history that there would be a significant number of Forever War veterans still young enough to fight.

The group mind of Man had surely made the same observation.

Sooz brought us more tea and went back to tell the others that our little mud lake had frozen solid. So there was no more time for paranoia. But the seed had been planted.

We unrolled two crossed layers of insulation sheet, and then went about the odd business of actually raising the barn.

The floor was the easy part: slabs of foamsteel rectangles that weighed about eighty kilograms apiece. Two big people or four average ones could move one with ease. They were numbered 1–40; we just picked them up and put them down, aligned with the stakes we agnostics had pounded in.

This part was a little chaotic, since all thirty people wanted to work at once. But we did eventually get them down in proper order.

Then we all sat and watched while the mastic was poured in. The boards that had served as forms for the frozen mud did the same for the mastic. Po and Eloi Casi used long, broom-like things to push the grey mastic around as it oozed out of the truck. It would have settled down into a level surface eventually, but we knew from experience that you could save an hour or so by helping the process along. When it was about a handspan deep, and level, Man flipped a switch and it turned into something like marble.

That's when the hard work started. It would have been easy with a crane and a front-end loader, but Man was proud of having designed these kits so they could be put up by hand, as a community project. So no big machines came along with them, unless it was an emergency.

(In fact, this was the *opposite* of an emergency: the Larsons wouldn't have much to put into the barn this year, their grapes almost destroyed by too much rain.)

Every fourth slab had square boxes on either end, to accept vertical girders. So you fasten three girders together, ceiling and wall supports, put a lot of glue into the square boxes, and haul them into an upright position. With the pressor field on, when they get within a degree or so of being upright, they snap into place.

After the first one was set, the rest were a little easier, since you could throw three or four ropes over the rigid uprights and pull the next threesome up.

Then came the part of the job that called for agile young people with no fear of heights. Our Bill and Sara, along with Matt Anderson and Carey Talos, clambered up the girders—not hard, with the integrated hand- and toe-holds—and stood on board scaffolds while hauling up the triangular roof trusses. They slapped glue down and jiggled the trusses until the pressor field snapped them into place. When that was done, they had the easier job of gluing and stapling down the roof sheets. Meanwhile, the rest of us glued and stapled the outer walls, and then unrolled thick insulation, and forced it into place with the inner walls. The window modules were a little tricky, but Marygay and Cat figured them out, working in tandem, one inside and one outside.

We "finished" the interior in no time, since it was all modular, with holes in the walls, floor, and roof girders that would snap-fit with pre-measured parts. Tables, storage bins and racks, shelves—I was actually a little jealous; *our* utility building was a jerry-built shack.

Eloi Casi, who loves working with wood, brought a wine rack that would hold a hundred bottles, so the Larsons could put some away each good year. Most of us brought something for the party; I had thirty fish thawed and cleaned. They weren't too bad, grilled with a spicy sauce, and the Bertrams had towed over their outdoor grill, with several armloads of split wood. They fired it up when we started working on the inside, and by the time we were done it was good glowing coals. Besides our fish, there was chicken and rabbit and the large native mushrooms.

I was too tired and dirty to feel much like partying, but there was warm water to scrub with, and Ami produced a few liters of skag she'd distilled, which had been sitting for months with berries, to soften the flavor. It was still fiery, and revived me.

The usual people had brought musical instruments, and they actually sounded pretty good in the big empty barn. People with some energy left danced on the new marble floor. I tended the fish and mushrooms and broiled onions, and drank almost enough skag to start dancing myself.

Man declined our food, politely, and made a few stress measurements, and declared the barn safe. Then she went home to do whatever it is they do.

Charlie and Diana joined me at the grill, setting out chicken pieces as I removed fish.

"So you'd fight them?" she said quietly. Charlie'd been talking to her. "To what end? If you killed every one of them, what would it accomplish?"

"Oh, I don't want to kill even one of them. They're people, whatever else they claim to be. But I'm working on something. I'll bring it up at a meeting when we have the bugs ironed out."

"We? You and Marygay?"

"Sure." Actually, I hadn't discussed it with her, since the thought had only occurred to me between the mastic and the girders. "One for one and all for all."

"You had some strange sayings in the old days."

"We were strange people." I carefully loosened the grilled fish and slipped them onto a warm platter. "But we got things done."

Marygay and I talked long into the night and early morning. She was almost as fed up as I was, with Man and our one-sided arrangement, breeding stock staked out on this dead-end arctic planet. It was survival, but only that. We should do more, while we were still young enough.

She was wildly enthusiastic about my scheme at first, but then had reservations because of the children. I was pretty sure I could talk them into going along with the plan. *At least Sara,* I thought privately.

She agreed that we ought to work out some details before we brought the thing to meeting. Not present it to the kids until after we'd talked it over with the other vets.

I didn't sleep until almost dawn, blood singing with revolution. For several weeks we tried to act normal, stealing an hour here and there to take a notebook out of hiding and jot down thoughts, work on the numbers.

forever free

In retrospect, I think we should have trusted Bill and Sara to be in on it from the first. Our judgment may have been clouded by the thrill of shared secrecy, and the anticipated pleasure of dropping a bombshell.

three

B y sundown the rain had gone through sleet to soft sifting snow, so we let Bill go straight to his volleyball game, and walked over to Charlie's. Selena, the larger moon, was full, and gave the clouds a pleasant and handy opalescence. We didn't need the flashlight.

Their place was about a klick from the lake, in a copse of evergreens that looked disconcertingly like palm trees on Earth. Palm trees heavy with snow sort of summed up Middle Finger.

We'd called to say we were coming early. I helped Diana set up the samovars and tea stuff while Marygay helped Charlie in the kitchen.

(Diana and I had a secret sexual history that not even she knew about. Conventionally lesbian before she came here, during Sade-138 she had gotten drunk and made a pass at me, just to give it a try the old-fashioned way. But she passed out before either of us could do anything about it, and didn't remember it in the morning.)

I lifted the iron kettle of boiling water and poured it over the leaves in two pots. Tea was one thing that adapted well to this planet. The coffee was no better than army soya. There was no place on the planet warm enough for it to grow naturally.

I put the heavy kettle back down. "So your arm's better," Diana observed. She'd given me an elastic thing and some pills, after I pulled a muscle working on the roof.

"Haven't lifted anything heavier than a piece of chalk."

She punched a timer for the tea. "You use *chalk*?"

"When I don't need holo. The kids are kind of fascinated by it."

"Any geniuses this term?" I taught senior physics at the high school and Introduction to Mathematical Physics at the college.

"One in college, Matthew Anderson. Leona's boy. Of course I didn't have him in high school." Gifted science students had classes taught by Man. Like my son. "Most of them, I just try to keep awake."

Charlie and Marygay brought in trays of cheese and fruit, and Charlie went out to get another couple of logs for the fire.

Their place was better suited than ours, or most others', for this sort of thing. Downstairs was one large round room, the kitchen in a separate alcove. The building was a metal dome that had been half of a Tauran warship's fuel tank, doors and windows cut in, its industrial origin camouflaged inside with wooden paneling and drapes. A circular staircase led to the bedrooms and library upstairs. Diana had a small office and examination room up there, but she did most of her work in town, at the hospital and the university clinic.

The fireplace was a raised circle of brick, halfway between

the center and wall, with a conical hood. So the fire was sort of like a primitive campfire, a nice locus for a meeting of a council of elders.

Which is what this was, though the ages of the participants ranged from over a thousand to barely a hundred, depending on when they were drafted into the Forever War. Their physical age went from late thirties to early fifties, in Earth years. The years here were three times as long. I guess people would eventually become used to the idea of starting school at 2, puberty before 4, majority at 6. But not my generation.

I had been physically 32 when I got here, although if you counted from birth date, ignoring time dilation and collapsar jumps, I was 1,168 in Earth years. So I was 54 now—or "32 plus 6," as some vets said, trying to reconcile the two systems.

The vets began to arrive, by ones, twos, and fours. Usually about fifty showed up, about a third of those within walking distance. One was an observer, with a holo recorder, who came from the capital city, Centrus. Our veterans' group had no name, and no real central organization, but it did keep records of these informal meetings in an archive the size of a marble.

One copy was in a safe place and the other was in the pocket of the woman with the recorder. Either one would scramble itself if touched by Man or Tauran; a film on the outside of the marble sensed DNA.

It wasn't that a lot of secret or subversive discussion went on here; Man knew how most of the vets felt, and didn't care. What could we do?

For the same reason, only a minority of the vets ever came to the meetings, and many of them just came to see friends. What was the use of griping? You couldn't change anything. Not everyone even believed things needed changing.

They didn't mind being part of a "eugenic baseline." What I called a human zoo. When one Man died, another was quickened, by cloning. Their genetic makeup never changed—why mess with perfection? Our function was to go ahead and make babies the old-fashioned way, random mutation and evolution. I suppose if we came up with something better than Man, they'd start using our genetic material instead. Or perhaps see us as dangerous rivals and kill us off.

But meanwhile we were "free." Man had helped us start up a civilization on this planet, and kept us in touch with the other inhabited ones, including Earth. You could even have gone to Earth, when you mustered out, if you were willing to pay the price—be sterilized and become one of them.

A lot of vets had done it, but Earth didn't sound at all inviting to me. One big city, full of Man and Taurans. I could live with these long winters, for the sake of the company.

Most of the people were reasonably content here. I was hoping to change that tonight. Marygay and I had been hatching a plan, and I was going to throw it out for discussion.

After about a half-hour, forty people had shown up, clustered around the fire, and I supposed weather was keeping the rest away. Diana tapped on a glass for attention, and introduced the woman from Centrus.

Her name was Lori. Her English had the flat Man accent of most Centrans. (All of us vets spoke English, which had been the default language during the Forever War, for people born centuries and continents—or even planets—apart. Some of us only spoke it at get-togethers like this, and the strain showed.)

She was small and slender and had an interesting tattoo that peeked out from under her singlet, a snake with an apple in its mouth. "There's not much to report that hasn't been in the news," she said. "A number of Taurans landed and stayed for one day of meetings, evidently some sort of delegation. But they never appeared in public."

"Good thing," Max Weston said. "I don't care if I never see one of those bastards again."

"Don't come to Centrus, then. I see one or two a day, in their bubbles."

"That's gutsy," he admitted. "Sooner or later somebody'll take a shot at them."

"That may be their purpose," I said. "Decoys, sacrificial lambs. Find out who has the weapons and the anger."

"Could well be," Lori said. "They don't seem to do much but walk around."

"Tourists," Mohammed Morabitu said. "Even Taurans might be tourists."

"Three are permanent," Cat said. "A friend of mine installed a heat pump in their apartment in the Office for Interplanetary Communications."

"Anyhow," Lori said, "these Taurans came in for a day, were put on a blacked-out floater from the Law Building, spent four hours there, and returned to the shuttle and left. A couple of cargo handlers saw them; otherwise they could have been in and out without being noticed by humans."

"I wonder why bother with secrecy," I said. "There've been delegations before."

"I don't know. And the shortness of the visit was odd, as well as the number four. Why should a group mind send more than one representative?"

"Redundancy," Charlie said. "Max might have run into them and killed three with his bare hands."

As far as we could tell, the Tauran "group mind" was no

more mysterious than Man's. No telepathy or anything; individuals regularly uploaded and downloaded experiences into a common memory. If an individual dies before tapping into the Memory Tree, new information is lost.

It did seem uncanny, since they were all physically twins. But we could do the same thing, if we were willing to have holes drilled into our skulls and plugs installed. Thanks, no. I have enough on my mind.

"Otherwise," Lori continued, "not much is happening in Centrus. The force field bunch got voted down again, so we'll be shoveling snow another year."

Some of us laughed at that—with only ten thousand people, Centrus wasn't big enough to warrant the energy expenditure to maintain a winter-long force field. But it *was* the planetary capital, and some citizens wanted the field as a status symbol as much as a convenience. Having the only spaceport, and alien visitors, didn't make them special enough.

To my knowledge, no Taurans had ever been here to Paxton. It might be unsafe; with our large vet population, a lot of people were like Max, unforgiving. I didn't bear them any animus myself. The Forever War had been a colossal misunderstanding, and perhaps we were more at fault than they.

They were still ugly and smelled weird and had killed a lot of my friends. But it wasn't *Taurans* who had sentenced us to life imprisonment on this iceberg. That was Man's idea. And Man might be a few billion twins, but they were still biologically human.

A lot of what went on in these meetings was just a more splenetic version of complaints that had already been sent through channels. The power grid was unreliable and *had* to be fixed before deep winter, or people would die, and the only response from Centrus was a schedule of municipal engineering priorities, where we kept getting shoved back in favor of towns that were closer to the capital. (We were the farthest away—a sort of Alaska or Siberia, to use examples that would be meaningless to almost everyone.)

Of course, the main reason for these secret meetings was that Centrus did not really reflect our concerns or serve our needs. The government was human, elected representatives whose numbers were based on population and profession. But in actual administration, Man had oversight that amounted to veto power.

And Man's priorities were not the same as ours. It was more than just a city/country thing, even though it sometimes took that appearance. I called it "deliberate speciation." About half the population of Men on the planet lived in Centrus, and most of the ones sent out to places like Paxton usually only stayed one long Year before going back. So whatever benefited Centrus benefited Man. And weakened us, out in the provinces, however indirectly.

I'd worked with Man teachers, of course, and a few times dealt with administrators. I'd long gotten over the uncanniness of them all looking and, superficially, acting the same. Always calm and reasonable, serious and gentle. With just a grain of pity for us.

We talked about the grid problem, the school problems, the phosphate mine that they wanted to build too close to Paxton (which would also bring a freight monorail that we needed), and smaller problems. Then I dropped my bombshell.

"I have a modest proposal." Marygay looked at me and smiled. "Marygay and I think we all should help Man and our Tauran brothers out with their noble experiment."

There was a moment of absolute silence, except for the crackling fire. The phrase "modest proposal" meant nothing to most of them, I realized, born a millennium after Swift. "Okay," Charlie said. "What's the punch line?"

"They want to isolate a human population as a genetic baseline. Let's give them isolation with a vengeance.

"What I propose is that we take the *Time Warp* from them. But we don't just go back and forth between Mizar and Alcor. We take it out as far as it can go, and come back safely."

"Twenty thousand light-years," Marygay said. "Forty thousand, here and back. Give them two thousand generations for their experiment."

"And leave us alone for two thousand generations," I said.

"How many of us could you take?" Cat asked.

"The *Time Warp*'s designed for two hundred, crowded," Marygay said. "I spent a few years on it, waiting for William, and it wasn't too bad. We would probably want a hundred fifty, for long-term living."

"How long?" Charlie said.

"We'd age ten years," I said. "Real years."

"It's an interesting idea," Diana said, "but I doubt you'd have to *highjack* the damned thing. It's a museum piece, empty for a generation. Just ask for it."

"We shouldn't even have to ask for it. Man's claim to ownership of it is a legal fiction. *I* paid for one three-hundred-twelfth of it, myself," Marygay said. There were 312 vets in on the original "time shuttle" deal.

"With wealth artificially generated by relativity," Lori said. "Your salary piling up interest, while you were out soldiering."

"That's true. It was still money." Marygay turned to the others. "Nobody else here bought a piece of the shuttle?"

There was a general shaking of heads, but Teresa Larson raised her hand. "They stole it from us, pure and simple," she said. "I got billions of Earth dollars, enough to buy a mansion on the Nile. But it won't buy a loaf of bread on Middle Finger."

"To be devil's advocate here," I said, "Man offered to 'assume stewardship' of it, if the humans were going to abandon it. And most of the humans had no interest in it after it had served its purpose."

"Including me," Marygay said. "And I don't deny having been a willing collaborator in the swindle. They bought back our shares with money we could only spend on Earth. It was amusing at the time, worthless money in exchange for a worthless antique."

"It *is* an antique," I said. "Marygay took me up there once to show me around. But did it ever occur to you to wonder *why* they keep it maintained?"

"Tell me," Diana said. "You're going to."

"Not out of sentiment, that's for sure. I suspect they're maintaining it as a kind of lifeboat for themselves, if the situation gets difficult."

"So let's *make* it difficult," Max said. "Stack 'em in there like cordwood and shoot 'em back to Earth. Or to their Tauran pals."

I ignored that. "No matter what their plans are, they won't just let us have it. It may be three Earth centuries old, but it's still by far the largest and most powerful machine in this corner of the universe—even without weapons, a Class III cruiser is a lot of power and materiel. They don't make anything like them anymore. It probably comprises a tenth of the actual material wealth in the system."

"It's an interesting thought," Lori said, "but how do you plan to get there? Both of the orbital shuttles on the planet are at Centrus. You'll have to highjack at least one of those before you highjack the time shuttle."

"It will take some planning," I admitted. "We have to manufacture a situation where the alternative to letting us take the *Time Warp* is unacceptable. Suppose we had kidnapped those four Taurans and threatened to kill them?"

She laughed. "They'd probably say, 'Go ahead,' and send for four more."

"I'm not convinced of that. I suspect they may be no more actually interchangeable than Man is. We only have their word for it—as you say, if they're all the same, why go to the expense of sending four?"

"You could just ask them for the ship first," said Ami Larson. "I mean, they *are* reasonable. If they said no, then—"

People were murmuring, and a couple of them laughed out loud. Ami was third-generation Paxton, not a vet. She was here because she was married to Teresa.

"You grew up with them, Ami." Diana kept a controlled neutral expression. "Some of us old folks aren't so trusting."

"So we go out for ten years, or forty thousand, and come back," said Lar Po. "Suppose Man's experiment has been successful. We'll be useless Cro-Magnons."

"Worse than that," I said cheerfully. "They'll probably have directed their evolution into some totally new direction. We might be like house pets. Or jellyfish.

"But part of my point is that you and I and most of us here have done this before. Every time we came back from a campaign, we'd have to start over—even if only a few dozen years had passed on Earth, most of our friends and relatives had died or aged into totally different people. Customs and laws were alien. We were largely unemployable, except as soldiers."

"And you want to do it again, voluntarily?" Charlie said. "Leave behind the life you've built for yourself?"

"Fisherman-teacher. I could tear myself away."

"William and I are in a better situation than most," Marygay said. "Our children are grown, and we're still young enough to strike out in a new direction."

Ami shook her head. She was our age, biologically, and she and Teresa had teenage daughters. "You aren't curious about how your kids will turn out? You don't want to see your grand-children?"

"We're hoping they'll come along," she said.

"If they don't?"

"Then they don't," I said. "A lot of children leave home and start off on their own."

Ami pressed on. "But not many parents do. Look at the choice you're giving them. Throw away their own world to join their parents."

"As time travelers. As pioneers."

Charlie butted in. "Forget about that aspect for a minute. Do you actually think you can recruit a hundred, a hundred fifty people without anybody going to Man and pointing the finger at you?"

"That's why we want to keep it among vets."

"I just don't want to see my oldest friend in jail."

"We're *in* jail, Charlie." I made a gesture that didn't knock anything over. "We can't see the bars because they're over the horizon."

The meeting broke up at midnight, after I called for a show of hands. Sixteen were with us, eighteen against, and six undecided. More support than I'd thought.

We walked home through snow that had a pleasant crunch to it, enjoying the night air, not saying much.

We came in the back door, and there at the dining room table, sipping tea, was Man. Over by the fire, warming its back, a Tauran. My arm came up halfway, in an aiming reflex.

"It's late," I said to the Man, my eyes on the Tauran's fisheye clusters. One hand fluttered its seven fingers, fourteen-jointed.

"I have to talk to you now."

"Where are the children?"

"I asked them to go upstairs."

"Bill! Sara!" I called. "Whatever you say to us, they can hear."

I turned to the Tauran. "—An evening of good fortune," I approximated in its language. Marygay repeated it, better.

"Thank you," it said in English, "but not for you, I fear." It was wearing a black cloak, a nice Hallowe'en effect with its wrinkled orange skin. The cloak made it look less alien, hiding the wasp waist and huge pelvis.

"I must be getting old," I said to Man. "Lori seemed like one of us."

"She is. She didn't know we were listening."

Bill and Sara were at the top of the stairs in nightgowns. "Come on down. We're not going to say anything you can't hear."

"But I am," Man said. "Go back to bed." They obeyed.

Disappointing, but not surprising. They'd listen anyhow.

"This is Antres 906," Man said, "the cultural attaché to Middle Finger."

I nodded at it. "Okay."

"Are you curious as to why he is here?"

"Not really. Just go ahead and have your say."

"He is here because a Tauran representative must be present in any negotiations involving possible travel to Tauran planets."

"What does that have to do with culture?" Marygay said.

"Pardon me?"

"It's the cultural attaché," she said. "What does that have to do with us borrowing the time shuttle?"

" 'Culture' includes tourism. And stealing is not borrowing."

"They're not on our route," I said. "We're going straight up, out of the galactic plane, and straight back. An isosceles triangle, actually."

"You should have gone through proper channels for this."

"Sure. Starting with you, the sheriff." He covered the back of his hand, with its identifying scar.

"You could start with anyone. We *are* a group mind."

"But you didn't send just anyone. You sent the one Man in this town who has weapons and exercises with weights."

"You are both soldiers." He opened his vest to display a large pistol. "You might resist."

"Resist what?" Marygay said.

"Coming with me. You're under arrest."

Paxton doesn't have a large enough criminal element to warrant an actual jail, but I suppose anything that locks on the outside will do. I was in a white room with no windows, furnished with a mattress on the floor and a toilet. There was a fold-down sink next to the toilet, and across from it, a fold-down desk. But no chair. The desk had a keyboard, but it didn't work.

It had a barroom smell, spilled alcohol. That must be what they used as a disinfectant, for some reason.

I knew from a visit last year that the place had only two detention rooms, so Marygay and I constituted a crime wave. (Serious criminals, actually, didn't even spend the night here; they went straight to the real jail in Wimberly.)

I spent a while contemplating the error of my ways, and then managed to get a few hours' sleep in spite of not being able to turn off the lights.

When the sheriff opened the door I could see sunshine behind him; it was ten or eleven. He handed me a white cardboard box that had soap, a toothbrush, and such. "The shower is across the hall. Please join me for tea when you are ready." He left with no further explanation.

There were two showers; Marygay was already in one of them. I raised my voice. "He tell you anything?"

"Just unlocked the door and said to come for tea. Why didn't we ever think of doing this with the children?"

"Too late to start now." I showered and shaved and we went to the sheriff's office together.

His pistol was hanging on a peg behind him. The papers on his desk had been hastily stacked in a corner, and he'd set out a pot of tea with some crackers and jam and honey.

We sat and he poured us tea. He looked tired. "I've been with the Tree all night." Since it had become daytime in Centrus, he might have been with hundreds or a thousand Men. "I have a tentative consensus."

"That took all night?" I said. "For a group mind, you don't synapse very fast." I kidded my Man colleagues at the university about that. (Physics, in fact, was a good demonstration of Man's limitations: an individual Man could tap into my colleagues' brains, but he or she wouldn't understand anything advanced without having previously studied physics.)

"In fact, much of that time was waiting for individuals to be summoned. Besides your . . . problem, there was another important decision to be made, not unrelated. 'The more leaves, the more Tree.' "

The jam was greenberry, a spicy sour flavor I'd liked immediately—one of the only things that had impressed me, the first day on Middle Finger. I'd arrived in deep winter.

"So you've decided to hang us in the town square?" I said. "Or will it be a simple private beheading?"

"If it were necessary to kill you, it would already have been done." Great sense of humor. "What would be the point in explaining things?"

He poured himself some tea. "There will be a wait. I need confirmation from the Whole Tree." That meant sending word to Earth and back, at least ten months. "But the tentative consensus is to send you away with my blessings. Give you the time shuttle."

"And in return," Marygay said, "you lose one hundred fifty powerful malcontents."

"It's not just that. You are already fascinating anachronisms. Think of how valuable you will be forty thousand years from now!"

"Living fossils," I said. "What an idea."

He hesitated for a moment; the word was unfamiliar. There were no actual fossils on his world. "Yes, in body as well as in modes of thought. In a way, I owe it to my own heritage. I should have thought of it myself." In their own language, there was a "collective 'I,' " which I assumed he was using.

"You said there were two decisions," Marygay said. "A related one."

"A mirror of yours, in a way." He smiled. "You know I love humans very much. It has always saddened me to see you go through life crippled."

"Crippled . . . by our individuality?" I said.

"Exactly! Unable to tap the Tree, and share life with billions of others."

"Well, we were given the choice when we mustered out. I've had over twenty years to regret not joining you, and so far I'm just as glad I didn't."

"You did have the choice, yes, and some veterans took it."

"How many?" Marygay asked.

"Actually, less than one percent. But I was new and strange to you then.

"The point is that it's been a hundred Years—nearly three

hundred Earth years—since anyone was given the choice. The population of Middle Finger has grown in that time to over twenty thousand, more than large enough to maintain a viable genetic pool. So I want to start giving people the choice again."

"Anyone who wants can become you?" I had a powerful premonitory urge to gather my children to me.

"No, it would only be one per new birth, and they would have to pass tests for suitability. And they wouldn't really *be* me, of course; their genetic make-up will be inferior. But they would still be leaves on the Tree." He smiled in a way that I'm sure he thought was not condescending. "It sounds horrible to you, doesn't it. You call us 'zombies.' "

"It does occur to me that there are enough of you already, on this planet. Not to mention ten billion or so back on Earth. Why not leave us alone? That was the original plan."

"This is consistent with the original plan, only kinder. You don't see it that way because you're too old-fashioned."

"Well, at least we have ten months to get used to the idea." To talk some sense into Bill and Sara.

"Oh, this isn't like the starship. I can go ahead, and if the Whole Tree disagrees, only few people will be affected. But I do know myself; I know the Tree. There will be no problem."

"People who join you will still be human, though," Marygay said. "They'll still marry and have families."

Man looked puzzled. "Of course not."

"But they'll be able," I said.

"Oh, no. They will have to consent to sterilization." He shook his head. "You don't understand. You say there are enough of me. In reality, there are more than enough of *you*."

I went straight from jail to the university, since I had to teach at 1400, and liked to be in the office for an hour before class, to go over notes and be available to talk to students. They served a hot lunch in the teachers' lounge, too.

It was kind of grandiose to call the place a "university," though it did grant a couple of dozen degrees. It was a circle of ten log buildings connected by breezeways. My physics building had two labs, two small classrooms, and a larger lecture hall, which we shared with chemistry and astronomy. The second floor, which was really just a high attic, was a storage area with two offices tacked on the end.

I shared the office with a Man and Jynn Silver. Jynn had not been at the meeting, because she'd gone to Centrus for her son's wedding, but I was pretty sure she would be on our side.

She had no love for Man in general, and for the one who shared our office, in particular.

He was there when I came in, after a quick bowl of soup at the lounge. That was odd; he taught mornings and didn't usually hang around.

He was staring out the window. "You know," he said without preamble. "You're one of the first to know that you might join us. Rather than leave us."

"True." I sat down and turned on my screen. "I was tempted for about a microsecond. Then sanity returned."

"Joking aside. You should take some time to consider the advantages."

"I'm not joking." I looked over at him. "To me it would be a kind of death."

"The death of your individuality." He pronounced the last word very slowly, with just a breath of contempt.

"It's not something you could really understand. Human thing."

"I'm human." Technically true. "If you wanted more children, you could adopt."

Now *there* was a compelling argument. "Two's plenty, thanks." I blinked through the index outline.

"You could save so much research time—"

"I'm not *doing* research. I'm a modest fisherman who's trying to teach rotational kinematics. If you'll let me get to my notes."

"Sorry."

There was a light knock on the doorframe. "Master Mandella?"

Baril Dain, from last term. "Come on in, Baril."

He glanced at Man. "I don't want to take up your time. Just that, well, I heard about your time trip thing. Can anyone go?"

"We'll have to pick from volunteers." He'd been a below-average student, but I'd made allowance for home conditions. His mother a drunk and his father living over in Filbin. "Are you six yet?"

"I will be in Archimedes, 13 Archimedes."

"That'll be plenty of time." Six months. "We'll need young people. What are you best at?"

"Music. I don't remember your word, the English word for it . . . the choséd-reng."

"Harp," Man supplied, not looking up. "Forty-four-string magnetoharmonic neoharp."

God, I hated the whining sound of those. "We'll see. We'll need all kinds of talents." Probably human music would have priority, though.

"Thank you, sir." He nodded and backed out, as if I were still his teacher.

"The children know already," Man said. "I'm surprised."

"Good news travels fast." I opened a drawer with a screech and took out a pad and stylus, and pretended to copy something from the screen.

The classroom was stuffy, stale with three classes' exhalations. I opened the window partway and sat on the table in front. All twelve students were there.

A pretty girl in front raised her hand. "What's it like to be in jail, Master?"

"As many years as you've been in school, Pratha, you know all there is to know about jail." That got a slight laugh. "It's just a room with no windows." I picked up the text and brushed the face with my sleeve.

"Were you scared, Master?" Modea, my best pupil.

"Of course. Man isn't accountable to us. I could have been locked up forever, eating the slop they and you call food." They smiled indulgently at my old-fashionedness. "Or they could have executed me."

"Man wouldn't, sir."

"I guess you know them better than I do. But the sheriff was careful to point out that that was in their power." I held up the text. "Let's go back for a minute and review what we know about the big I, moment of inertia."

It was a difficult period. Rotational kinematics is not intuitive. I remembered how much trouble I'd had with it, more than halfway back to Newton's day. The kids paid attention and took notes, but most of them had that "on autopilot" look. Taking it down by rote, hoping they could puzzle it out later. Some of them would not. (Three were hopelessly lost, I suspected, and I'd have to talk to them soon.)

We ground through to the end of the lesson. While they were putting on their coats and capes, Gol Pri voiced an obvious concern. "Master Mandella, if Man does let you take the starship, who will our teacher be? For mathematical physics?"

I thought for a moment, discarding possibilities. "Man, probably, if it's someone from Paxton." Gol's face tightened slightly. He'd had classes from my officemate. "I would put in a search, though. There are plenty of people in Centrus who could do it, if they felt a sudden hunger for life on the frontier."

"Would you be teaching on the ship?" Pratha said. "If we came along?"

Her expression was interesting and not ambiguous. Down, boy; she's barely older than your daughter. "Sure. That's about all I'm good for."

Actually, they might make me harvest fish, aboard the *Time Warp*. That would be a major part of the diet, and I certainly knew my way around a cleaver.

When I got home from class, I didn't go straight out to the dock. There was no rush. The day was clear and cold, Mizar making the sky a naked energetic blue, like an electric arc. I'd wait for Bill to get home.

Meanwhile I brewed a pot of tea and blinked through the news. The service came from Centrus, so our story was there, but buried in the exurb section, cross-ref to vets and Earth. Just as well. I didn't want a lot of questions before we had answers.

I asked for random Beethoven and just listened, staring out at the lake and forest. There was a time when I would have thought you'd be nuts to trade this for the austerity and monotony of a starship.

There was also a time when I was, we were, romantic about the frontier. We came out here when Marygay was pregnant with Bill. But it's grown up to where it's just Centrus without conveniences. And there's noplace farther out, not to live. No population pressure to speak of. No cultural mandate to keep moving out.

One of the useless things I remember from school is the Turner Thesis. How the American character was shaped by the frontier, always receding, always tempting.

That gave me a little chill. Is that what we were proposing?

A temporal version of a dream that was really dead before I was born. Though it drove my father, along with my family—in a VW bus with flowers painted all over the rusted body—to the Pacific and then north to Alaska. Where we found rough-and-ready frontier shops that served latte and cappuccino.

It was possible that out of ten billion souls scattered through this corner of the Galaxy, only Marygay and I had even a tenuous connection to the American frontier. Charlie and Diana and Max were born in a place that still called itself America, but it had not been a place that Frederick Jackson Turner would have recognized, its only "frontier" light-years and centuries away, men and women fighting an incomprehensible enemy for no reason.

Bill came in and we both put on aprons and gloves and went out to the dock. We worked in relative silence, monosyllables, for the first two trotlines, Bill beheading them with such fervor that twice he got the cleaver stuck in the wood.

"People give you shit about your parents being jailbirds?"

" 'Birds'? Oh, being in jail, yeah. They mostly thought it was funny. Stealing the starship and all, like a movie."

"Looks like they'll just give it to us."

"Our history Man said she thought they would. They could replace the starship with a newer one, from Earth, through the collapsar. No real loss." He whacked down on a fish. "To them."

That was clear enough. "But there would be to you. If you don't go with us."

He held down the writhing headless fish for a moment, then chopped off its tail and threw it in the freezer. "There are things I can't say in English. Maybe there aren't words."

"Go on."

"You say 'there would be to you,' a loss. Or you could say 'there *will* be a loss to you.' But nothing in between."

I paused, my hand on the line, trying to sort out grammar. "I don't get it. You say 'would' because it's in the future, uncertain."

He spat out a phrase in Standard: "*Ta meeya a cha!* You say *meeya* when the outcome is uncertain but the decision has been made. Not *ta loo a cha* or *ta lee a cha*, which is like your 'would' or 'will.' "

"I was never good with languages."

"I guess not. But the point is, the point is . . ." He was angry, jaw set, reddening. He did another fish and jammed its head back on the hook. "No matter what the outcome, you've done it. You've said to the world 'the hell with Bill and Sara.' You're going your own way. Whether Man allows it or not, the intent is there."

"That's harsh." I finished the fish I was doing. "You can come with us. I *want* you to come with us."

"And what an offer that is! Throw away everything! Thanks a lot."

I struggled to keep my voice calm. "You could see it as an opportunity, too."

"Maybe to you. I'd be over ten—thirty-some, by little years—and everyone I ever knew, except for you, dead for forty thousand. That's not an opportunity. That's a *sentence!* Almost a death sentence."

"To me it's a frontier. The only one left."

"Cowboys and Hindus," he said quietly, turning back to the fish. I didn't say "Pakistanis."

I could see that he was normal and I was not, even by the standards of my own long-dead culture. Marygay and I, and the other Forever War vets, had repeatedly been flung forward in time, often knowing that when you came to ground, the only people still alive from your past would be the ones you had traveled with.

Twenty years later, that was still central to me: the present is a comforting illusion, and although life persists, any one life is just a breath in the wind. I would be challenged on that the next afternoon, from an unexpected source.

Three times a long Year, I had to report to Diana for some primitive medicine. No human or Man born in the past several centuries had had cancer, but some of us fossils lacked the genes to suppress it. So periodically, Diana had to check, as we politely used to say, where the sun don't shine.

The wall of her office, upstairs in the dome, had been gleaming metal at first, with really strange acoustics due to its roundness. She could stand across the room and whisper, and it would sound as if she were next to your ear. Charlie and Max and I liberated some studs and panels from a stack behind the firehouse, and nailed together a passably square room. The walls were a comfortable clutter of pictures and holos now, which I tried to study intensely as she threaded a sensor probe up into my colon.

"Your little friend's back," she said. "Precancerous lesions.

I've got a sample to send off." It was an odd sensation when the probe withdrew, so fast it made me gasp. Relief and a little pain, an erotic shiver.

"You know the drill. When you get the pill, don't eat for twelve hours, take it, then two hours later, stuff yourself. Bread, mashed potatoes." She crossed over to the steel sinks of the lab module, carefully holding the ophidian probe away from her. "Get cleaned up and dressed while I set this up."

She would send the cells off to a place in Centrus, where they'd make up a pill full of mechanical microphages, programmed to dine on my cancer and then switch off. It was only a minor inconvenience, nothing compared to the skin cancer treatment, which was just painted on, but burned and itched for a long time.

Marygay and I had to chase cancer all the time, like everybody we knew who had gone through limb replacement on the hospital planet Heaven, back in the old days. They've licked that now.

I eased myself down by her desk just as she finished wrapping the package. She sat down and addressed it from memory. "I ordered five of these, which should be plenty for ten years. The examination's just a formality; I'd be surprised if your cancer's changed since the first one."

"You'll be along, though, to check it out?"

"Yeah. I'm as crazy as you are."

I laughed. She didn't. She put her elbows on the desk and stared at me. "I'll never bother you about this again, William, but as your doctor I have to say it."

"I think I know what it is."

"You probably do. This whole ambitious scheme is just an elaborate response to post–traumatic stress disorder. I could give you pills for that."

"As you've offered in the past. Thanks, but no thanks. I don't believe in chemical exorcism."

"Charlie and I are running away with you for the same reason. Hoping to put our ghosts to rest. But we're not leaving any children behind."

"Neither are we. Unless they choose to stay."

"They will. You're going to lose them."

"We have ten months to turn them around."

She nodded. "Sure. If you can get Bill to go, I'll let you stick something up *my* ass."

"Best offer I've had all day."

She smiled and put a hand on my arm. "Come on downstairs. Let's have a glass of wine."

seven

Marygay and I were in the group of twelve, plus one Man and one Tauran, who went up to inspect the starship, to determine what would be necessary for the voyage. We couldn't just turn the key and go, when the ten months were up. We were asssuming the Whole Tree would endorse the "good riddance" policy, and it could take most of the ten months' wait to get the ship in order.

The trip up to orbit was interesting, the first time I'd been in space since the kids were born. We went staight up, with constant gentle acceleration. That was a profligate waste of antimatter, I knew. The Man pilot shrugged and said there was plenty. She wasn't sure where it came from; maybe from the huge supply in the *Time Warp*.

For a spaceship, the shuttle was tiny, about the size of a schoolbus. There were windows all around, including behind, so we could watch Centrus shrink until it merged with the country-side. Ahead, the starship became the brightest star in the darkening sky. By the time we were in black space, you could tell it wasn't a star; slightly elongated.

The shuttle flipped and began slowing when we were maybe a thousand kilometers from it. Braking at about two gees, it was uncomfortable to crane around to watch the starship grow. But it was worth a stiff neck.

The *Time Warp* was an antique, but not by my standards! It had been designed and built more than a millennium after I'd left school. The last cruiser I'd fought in had been an ungainly collection of modules stacked around in a jumble of girders and cables. The *Time Warp* had a simple elegant form: two rounded cylinders, attached at front and rear, with a slab of shielding between them along the rear half, to soak up gamma rays. The metal was like delicate lace around the very end of the top cylinder, where the antimatter engine waited.

We docked with an almost imperceptible bump, and when the airlock door irised open, my ears popped and I was suddenly glad they'd warned us to bring sweaters.

The ship had been maintained with the life-support systems at a bare minimum. The air was stale and cold, just enough above zero to keep the water from freezing and bursting pipes.

The partial pressure was equivalent to three kilometers' altitude, thin enough to make you dizzy. We would get used to it over time.

We used handholds to crawl clumsily through the zero-gee into an elevator decorated with cheerful scenes fom Earth and Heaven.

The control room looked more like something that actually belonged in a spaceship. A long console with four swivel chairs.

When we entered, the control board glittered into life, indicator lights going through some warming-up sequence, and the ship spoke to us in a friendly baritone.

"I've been expecting you. Welcome."

"Our agricultural expert wants the place warmed up as soon as possible," Man said. "What kind of timetable can she expect?"

"About two days for hydroponics. Five before you ought to start planting in the dirt. For aquaculture, it depends on the species, of course. The water will be at least ten degrees everywhere in eight days."

"You have a greenhouse you can warm up?"

"For seedlings, yes. It's almost ready now."

Teresa looked at Man. "Why don't a couple of us stay up here and get some flats started. Be nice to have stuff growing as soon as possible."

"I'd like to help," Rubi said. "Have to be back by the twenty-first, though."

"Me, too," Justin said. "When's the next flight?"

"We can be flexible," Man said. "A week, ten days." She made the kissing sound that signaled the ship that she was talking to it. "You have plenty of food for three people?"

"Several years' worth, if they can survive emergency rations. Or I can activate the galley, and they can use up frozen food. It's very old, though."

Teresa smacked. "Do that. Let's save the emergency rations for emergencies."

I wouldn't have minded joining them myself, though I'm not much of a farmer. It was pleasantly exciting. Like putting twigs on the embers of a banked fire, and blowing gently to make the small flame that would start it over again.

But I had classes and fish to take care of. Maybe when classes were over next month, I could come up and help get the aquaculture started.

Marygay pinched my butt. "Don't even think about it. You've got classes."

"I know, I know." How long had we been reading each other's minds?

We took a holo tour of the "engine room," which was not a room by anybody's definition. It did have a cylindrical wall of lacy aluminum, for the convenience of workers. Nobody would ever be out there while the engine was running, of course. Gamma-ray leakage would fry them in seconds. A lot of the engine crew would practice working with remote robots, in case repairs had to be made and the engine couldn't be shut off.

There was a huge water tank—a drained lake's worth of water—and a much smaller glowing ball of antimatter, a perfect sphere of sparkling blue pinpricks.

I stared at it for some time, the ship droning on about technical specifications that I could look up later. That glittering ball was our ticket to a new life, one that suddenly seemed real. Freedom, in this small prison.

It had occurred to me that it wasn't just the bland tyranny of Man and Tauran that I wanted to escape. It was also everyday life, the community and family that I had watched growing for the past generation. I was dangerously close to becoming a tribal elder—and despite the fact that I *was* technically the oldest person on the planet, I wasn't nearly ready for that. Time and spirit for a couple of adventures more. Even a passive adventure like this.

Call it fear of becoming a grandfather. Settling into the role of observer and advisor. I shaved off my beard years ago, when it started to show patches of white. I could just see growing it long, sitting in a rocking chair on the porch . . .

Marygay wiggled my elbow. "Hello? Anybody home?" She laughed. "The ship wants to take us downstairs."

We wended our serpentine way back to the lift, and in my mind's eye I could almost see fields of grain and fruits and vegetables; the tanks roiling with fish and shrimp.

When we reached the midpoint we got out of the lift and followed Man, floating down the corridor lined with artwork that was showing age. We were out of practice with this kind of locomotion, and kept butting and nudging each other until, with the aid of handholds, we managed to stay in a more or less orderly line.

The "bottom" cylinder was the same size as the one we'd just left, but it looked larger, for the lack of things on a familiar human scale. Five escape craft dominated the cargo hold, each one a fighter modified to hold thirty people. They could only accelerate up to one-tenth the speed of light (and decelerate at the other end, of course), but the life-support equipment included suspended-animation tanks that would keep people somewhat alive for centuries. Mizar and Alcor are three light-years apart, so with the ship's original back-and-forth mission, the most time they would spend zipped up in the tanks was thirty years. Which would pass like nothing, supposedly.

I clicked for the ship's attention. "What's our upper limit, given the flight plan I filed? What's our point of no return?"

"It's not possible to be definite," it said. "Each suspended-animation tank will function until a vital component fails. They're superconducting, and require no power input, at least not for tens of thousands of years. I doubt that the systems would last more than a thousand years, though; a hundred light-years' distance. That will be a little more than three years into our voyage."

It was amusing that a machine would use a romantic word like "voyage." It was well programmed to keep company with a bunch of middle-aged runaways.

At the bow of the cylinder was a neat stack of modules left over from the war—a kind of build-a-planet kit, the ultimate lifeboat. We knew that earthlike worlds were common. If the ship couldn't make collapsar insertion and go home, those modules gave the people a chance of building a *new* home. We didn't know whether it had ever happened. There had been forty-three cruisers unaccounted for at the end of the war, some of them so far away that we would never hear from them. My own last assignment had been in the Large Magellanic Cloud, 150,000 light-years away.

Most of the rest of the hold was given over to redundancy, materials and tools to rebuild almost anything in the living cylinder, but the area closest to where we were floating was all tools, some as basic as picks and shovels and forklifts, some unrecognizably esoteric. If something went wrong with the drive or the life-support system, there would be no other job for anyone until it was fixed—or we were fried or frozen.

(Those of us with engineering and scientific backgrounds would be speed-training with the ALSC—Accelerated Life Situation Computer—which was not quite as good as learning in real time, hands on, but it did give you a lot of data, fast. It was sobering to realize that if something *did* go wrong with the drive—which restrained more energy than had been released in any Earth war—then the person in charge of repairing it would be essentially a walking, talking manual, who had really vivid memories of procedures that had actually been done by some actor centuries dead.)

On the way back up the corridor, Man showed off her zerogee expertise by exuberant spinning and cartwheeling. It was good to sometimes see them acting human.

We were free to wander around and poke at things for a couple of hours before going back to Centrus. Marygay and I retraced the patterns of her life here, but it seemed less like revisiting old memories than like exploring a ghost town.

We went into the last apartment she'd occcupied, waiting for me, and she said she wouldn't have recognized it. The last occupant had painted the walls in bright jagged graphics. When Marygay had lived there, the walls were light cobalt blue, and covered with her paintings and drawings. She didn't do it much anymore, but in the years while she was waiting here, she'd become an accomplished artist.

She'd looked forward to getting back to it, once the kids were out of the house. They might be *light-years* out of the house, soon.

"It's sad for you," I said.

"Yes and no. They weren't unhappy years. This was the stable part of my world. You'd make close friends and then they'd get off the ship, and every time you stopped at Middle Finger, they'd be six or twelve or eighteen years older, and then dead." She gestured at the dead dry fields and still waters. "This was permanence. That it's a shambles now does bother me a little."

"We'll have it rebuilt soon."

"Sure." She put her hands on her hips and surveyed the place. "We'll make it better."

eight

Of course, it wasn't going to be just a matter of rolling up our sleeves and slapping paint around. Man allotted us one shuttle every five days, so we had to plan carefully what and whom to take up when.

The "whom" was something we had to work out now. There were 150 slots to fill, and they couldn't just be random people. Marygay and Charlie and Diana and I all made up independent lists of the kinds of skills we'd need, and then met at our place and merged the lists and added a few more possibilities.

We had nineteen volunteers from Paxton—one had changed his mind after the meeting—and after we fit each of us to a job assignment, we publicized the plan and asked for volunteers planet-wide, to fill the other 131 berths.

In a week, we had 1,600 volunteers, mostly from Centrus. There was no way the four of us could interview all of them, so first we had to winnow through the applications. I took 238 who had technical occupations and Diana took 101 who were medical. We split the rest up evenly.

I wanted, at first, to give priority to veterans, but Marygay talked me out of it. That was more than half the volunteers, but it wasn't necessarily the most qualified half. The proportion of them who were congenital malcontents and troublemakers was probably high. Did we want to be locked up in a box with them for ten years?

But how could we tell which of the applicants might be unstable, on the basis of a few paragraphs? The people who said some version of "You've got to take me; Man is driving me crazy!" were just echoing my own sentiments, but they might also be revealing an inability to get along with others, which would make them bad company in our mobile prison.

Both Diana and Marygay had studied psychology in school, but neither claimed any expertise in the detection of loonies.

We narrowed the applications down to four hundred, and wrote back a form letter emphasizing the negative aspects of the ten-year joyride. Isolation, danger, privation. The absolute certainty of returning to a completely alien world.

About 90 percent of the people wrote back and said okay; I've already taken these things into consideration. We dropped the ones who didn't respond before the deadline, and scheduled holo interviews with the others.

We wanted to wind up with a list of two hundred, fifty of them being alternates, to be called if we lost people from death or cold feet. Marygay and I interviewed half, Charlie and Diana the other half. We gave a slight edge to married couples or people in some long-term relationship, but tried not to give het preference over home. You could argue that the more homosexuals, the better, since they were unlikely to add to the population. We couldn't handle more than a dozen, maybe twenty, children.

Charlie and Diana would take longer than Marygay and I, since Diana had to keep clinic hours. Marygay and I were in the twenty-day recess between semesters.

That also meant that Bill and Sara were home, underfoot. Sara spent a lot of time on her loom, trying to finish up a large rug before school started. Bill's big project for the twenty days was to talk us out of this insane quest.

"What're you running away from?" was his basic question. "You and Mom won't let go of that damned war, and we're going to lose you to it, centuries after it's over."

Marygay and I argued that we weren't running *away* from anything. We were taking a leap into the future. A lot of our volunteers were his age or a little older, who had also grown up with Man, but had a less sanguine view of them.

About two weeks into the recess, Bill and Sara dropped their separate bombshells. I'd spent a pleasant hour in the kitchen, fixing polenta and eggs with the last greens of the season, listening to Beethoven and enjoying not talking to strangers over the holo. Bill had set the table without being asked, which I should have recognized as a danger sign.

They ate in relative silence while Marygay and I talked about the day's interviews—mostly about the rejects, who made for better conversation than the sane, sober ones who passed the test.

Bill finished his plate and pushed it slightly away from him. "I passed a test today."

I knew what he was going to say, and it felt as if the heat had been sucked out of my body; out of the room. "The sheriff's test?"

"That's right. I'm going to become one of them. A Man."

"You didn't say anything about—"

"Are you surprised?" He stared at me like a stranger on a bus.

"No," I finally said. "I thought you might wait until we were gone." And not be so obviously a traitor, I kept myself from saying.

"You still have time to change your mind," Marygay said. "They're not starting the program until deep winter."

"That's true," Bill said without elaboration. It felt like he was halfway there already.

Sara had put down her knife and fork and was not looking at Bill. "I've decided, too."

"You're not old enough to take the test yet," I said, perhaps a little too firmly.

"Not that. I've decided to go with you. If there's room for me."

"Of course there is!" No matter who we have to leave behind.

Bill looked startled. "I thought you were going to—"

"There's plenty of time for that." She looked at her mother with pretty earnestness. "You think that Man will be long gone when you return. I think they'll still be here, in improved, evolved form. *That's* when I'll join them, and bring them all that I've learned and seen on the voyage." Then she looked at me with her dimpled open smile. "Will you take me, as a spy for the other side?"

"Of course I will." I looked at Bill. "We do have to take a Man or two. The family could stay together."

"You don't understand. You don't get it at all." He stood up. "I'm going to a new world, too. And I'm going tomorrow."

"You're leaving?" Marygay said.

"Forever," he said. "I can't stand this anymore. I'm going to Centrus."

There was a long silence. "What about the house?" I said. "The fish?" The plan had been for him to take it all over, when we left.

"You'll just have to find somebody else." He was almost shouting. "*I can't live here!* I have to get out and start over."

"You couldn't wait until—" I began.

"*No!*" He glared at me, struggling for words, and then just shook his head and left the table. We watched in silence as he threw on his cold-weather gear and went outside.

"You aren't surprised," Sara said.

"We talked this over," I said. "He was going to keep the place; do the trotlines."

"The hell with the fish," Marygay said quietly. "Don't you see we just lost him? Lost him for good." She didn't cry until we were upstairs.

I just felt numb. I realized I'd given him up a long time ago. It's easier to stop being a father than a mother.

book two

THE BOOK OF CHANGES

B ill only stayed in Centrus for two days. He came back, embarrassed at his outburst. There was still no way he was going to get aboard that starship, but he wasn't going to go back on his word; he'd take care of the fish as long as it was necessary.

I couldn't blame him for wanting to go his own way. Like father, like son. Marygay was happy at his return, but wistful and a little shaken. How many times would she have to lose her son?

We were headed for the big city ourselves, which provoked an odd association with my own boyhood.

An unimaginably long time ago, when I was seven or eight, my hippy parents spent the summer in a commune in Alaska. (That's when my brother was conceived, by somebody; my father always insisted he looked like him!)

It was a fun summer, a highlight of my childhood. We

puffed up the Alcan Highway in our old Deadhead Volkswagen bus, camping or stopping in little Canadian towns along the way.

When we got to Anchorage, it seemed huge, and for years after, whenever he told people about the trip, my father quoted the guidebook: If you fly into Anchorage from an American city of any size, it seems small and quaint. If you drive or ferry up through all the little villages, it seems like a teeming metropolis.

I always remembered that when I came into Centrus, which is smaller than Anchorage had been, a millennium and a half ago. My own life has adapted itself to the scale and pace of a village, so my first impression of Centrus is one of dizzying speed and neck-craning size. But I take a mental deep breath and re- member New York and London, Paris and Geneva—not to men- tion Skye and Atlantis, the fabulous pleasure cities that sucked away our money on Heaven. Centrus is a hick town that happens to be the biggest hick town within twenty light-years.

I held on to that thought when we came in to confer with Centrus administrators—which is to say, the world's—about our timetable for fixing up and crewing the *Time Warp.*

We'd hoped they could just rubber-stamp it. Fourteen of us had spent most of a week arguing over who was to do what, when. I could just see starting over and repeating the process, with the additional pressure of demands from Man.

We went all the way up to the tenth-floor penthouse office of the General Administration Building, and presented our plan to four Men, two male and two female, and a Tauran, who could have been any of three sexes. He turned out to be Antres 906, of course, the cultural attaché we had entertained at our house the night I earned my first entry on the police blotter.

The five of them read the three-page schedule in silence, while Marygay and I looked out over Centrus. There wasn't really

too much to see. Beyond the dozen or so square blocks of downtown, the trees were higher than the buildings; I knew there was
a good-sized town out there, but the dwellings and businesses
were hidden by evergreens, all the way out to the shuttle pad on
the horizon. The shuttles themselves weren't visible; both were
inside the launching tubes that rose out of the horizon mist like
smokestacks on an old-fashioned factory.

The one wall of this room that wasn't window featured ten
paintings, five each of human and Tauran manufacture. The
human ones were bland cityscapes in the various seasons. The
Tauran things were skeins and splotches of colors that clashed
so much they seemed to vibrate. I knew that some of them were
pigmented with body fluids. They were evidently prettier if you
could see into the ultraviolet.

At some subtle signal, they all set down their copies of the
schedule in unison.

"We have no objection to this as far as it goes," said the
leftmost Man. She betrayed her lack of telepathy by glancing
down the row; the others nodded slightly, including the Tauran.
"The days when you need both shuttles will be an inconvenience,
but we can plan around them."

" ' . . . as far as it goes'?" Marygay said.

"We should have told you this earlier," she said, "but it must
be obvious. We will require that you take two more passengers.
A Man and a Tauran."

Of course. We'd known about the Man, and should have
foreseen the Tauran. "The Man is not a big problem," I said.
"He or she can eat our food. But ten years of rations for a
Tauran?" I did a quick mental calculation. "That's an extra six
or eight tonnes of cargo."

"No, it is not a problem," Antres 906 rasped. "My metabolism can be altered to survive on your food, with a few grams of supplement daily."

"You can see the value of this to us," the Man said.

"Now that I think of it, of course," I said. "Both of your species may change somewhat in forty thousand years. You want a pair of time travelers as baselines."

Marygay shook her head slowly, biting her lower lip. "We'll have to change the makeup of the crew. No disrespect, Antres, but there are many veterans who could not tolerate your presence for ten hours, let alone ten years."

"And in any case, we can't guarantee your safety," I said. "Many of us were conditioned to kill your kind on sight."

"But they have all been de-conditioned," Man said.

I thought of Max, slated as assistant civil engineer. "With uneven success, I'm afraid."

"That is understood and forgiven," Antres said. "If that part of the experiment fails, then it fails." It turned to the last page of the report and tapped on the diagram of the cargo cylinder. "I can make a small place to live down here. That way your people will not be exposed to me often or involuntarily."

"That's workable," I said. "Send us a list of things you'll need, and we'll integrate them into the loading schedule."

The rest was formalities, having a small cup of strong coffee and a glass of spirits with the Men. The Tauran disappeared and came back in a few minutes with his list. They had obviously been prepared for us.

We didn't say anything about it until we were out of the building. "Damn. We should have foreseen that and beaten them to the punch."

"We should have," Marygay said. "Now we have to go back and deal with people like Max."

"Yeah, but it won't be someone like Max who kills the Tauran. It'll be someone who thinks he's over with the war. And then one day just loses it."

"Someone like you?"

"I don't think so. Hell, I'm not over the war. Bill says that's why I'm running away."

"Let's not think about the children." She put an arm around my waist and bumped me with her hip. "Let's go back to the hotel and *actively* not think about them."

After a pleasant interlude, we spent the afternoon shopping, for friends and neighbors as well as ourselves. Nobody in Paxton had a lot of money; we basically had a barter economy, with every adult getting a small check each month from Centrus. Sort of like the universal dole that was working so well, the last time we'd been on Earth.

It did work pretty well on Middle Finger, since nobody expected luxuries. On Earth, people had been almost uniformly poor, but surrounded by constant reminders of unattainable wealth. Out here everyone had about the same kind of simple life.

We pushed a cart down the brick sidewalk, consulting our list, and made about a half-dozen stops. Herbs, guitar strings and clarinet reeds, sandpaper and varnish, memory crystals, a paint set, a kilo of marijuana (Dorian liked it but was allergic to Sage's homegrown variety). Then we had tea at a sidewalk café and watched people go by. It was always a novelty to see all those faces you didn't recognize.

"I wonder what this will be like when we come back."

"Unimaginable," I said, "unless it's ancient rubble. You go back forty millenniums in human history and what do you have? Not even towns, I suppose."

"I don't know. Let's remember to look it up." On the street in front of us, a car banged into the rear of another one. The Men who were driving the vehicles got out and silently inspected the damage, which was slight, just a mark on a bumper. They nodded at each other and went back to their places.

"Do you think that was an accident?" Marygay said.

"What? Oh . . . possibly not. Probably." A staged lesson on how well they got along together. How well Man got along with himself. The coincidence of it happening in front of us was unlikely; there was little traffic.

We indulged in the services of a masseuse and masseur for the hour before we caught the bus back to Paxton.

When we got back, I punched up the library to find out what we were doing forty thousand years ago. We weren't even "us" yet; still late Neanderthal. They did have flint and stone tools. No evident language or art, except for simple petroglyphs in Australia.

What if Man, and people, were to develop characteristics as profound and basic as language and art—which they could share with us, perhaps, only to the extent that we can "talk" to dogs, or be amused by the smears a chimp will make with fingerpaints?

It seemed to me that it would certainly be one or the other: extinction or virtual speciation. Either way, the 150 of us would be totally alone. To rebuild the race or wither away, a useless anachronistic appendage.

I was going to keep that conclusion to myself. As if no one else would arrive at it. It would be Aldo Verdeur-Sims to first bring it up in public, or at least semi-public.

"We're going to seem as alien to them as the Taurans did to us," Aldo said, "if they do manage to survive forty thousand years, which I doubt."

It was called a "discussion group" in the first note we'd sent around, but in fact it was most of the people Marygay and I figured would be most active in setting up the project, if not actually running the ship. Sooner or later there would be some democratic process.

Besides us, it was Cat and Aldo, Charlie and Diana, Ami and Teresa, and a floating population that included Max Weston (his xenophobia notwithstanding), our Sara, Lar Po, and the Tens—Mohammed and one or two of his wives.

Po was a contrarian, in his polite way: express an opinion and watch his brain cells start grinding away. "You assume constant change," he said to Aldo, "but in fact Man claims perfection, and no need to change. They might enforce that among themselves, even for forty thousand years."

"But the humans?" Aldo said.

Po dismissed our race with a flick of his hand. "I don't think we'll survive two thousand generations. Most likely, we'll challenge Man and the Taurans and be crushed."

We were meeting, as usual, in our dining room/kitchen. Ami and Teresa had brought two big jugs of blackberry wine, sweet and fortified with brandy, and the discussion was more animated than usual.

"You're both underestimating humanity," Cat said. "What's *most* likely is that Man and the Taurans will stagnate, while humans evolve beyond them. When we come back, it may be only *Man* who's familiar. Our own descendants grown into something beyond understanding."

"All this optimism," Marygay said. "Can we get back to the diagram?"

Sara had drawn up a neat timetable, based on my notes and Marygay's, roughing out the whole thing from now till launch on one big sheet of paper. At least it had started out neat. For the first hour tonight, people had studied it and penciled in suggestions. Then the Larsons came with their jugs, and the meeting became more relaxed and conversational. But we did have to refine the timetable in order to firm up the launch schedule.

You could actually look at it as two linked timetables, and in fact there was a ruled line separating the two: before approval and after approval. For the next nine months, we were limited to two launches a week, and one of them had to be reserved for fuel shipment—a tonne of water and two kilograms of antimatter (which with its containment apparatus took up half the shuttle's payload).

being leaders of the band. We did come up with the idea, of course, but we both knew from our military experience that we weren't natural-born leaders. Twenty years' parenting and helping a small community grow had changed us—and twenty years of being the "oldest" people in the world. There were plenty of people older than us in actual aging, but nobody else who could remember life before the Forever War. So people came to us for advice because of this mostly symbolic maturity.

Most people seemed to assume that I was going to be the captain, when the time came. I wondered how many would be surprised when I stepped down in favor of Marygay. She was more comfortable with being an officer.

Well, being an officer had gotten her Cat. All I got was Charlie.

The meeting broke up before dark. The first heavy flakes of a long storm were drifting down. There would be more than half a meter on the ground by morning; people had livestock to manage, fires to kindle, children to worry about—children like Bill, out on the road in this weather.

Marygay had gone to the kitchen to make soup and scones and listen to music, while Sara and I sat at the dining room table and consolidated all of the scribblings on her once-neat chart into a coherent timetable. Bill called from the tavern, where he'd been in a pool tournament, and said he'd like to leave the floater there, if nobody needed it right away, and walk home. The snow was so dense in the air that headlights were useless. I said that was a good idea, not mentioning the slur in his speech that made it a doubly good idea.

He seemed sober when he got home, more than an hour later. He came in through the mudroom, laughing while he beat snow off his clothes. I knew how he felt—this kind of snow was a bitch to drive in, but wonderful for walking. The sound of it feathering down, the light touch on skin—nothing like the killer horizontal spikes of a deep winter blizzard. We'd have neither aboard ship, of course, but the lack of one seemed a more than fair trade for the other.

Bill got a fresh scone and some hot cider, and sat down with us. "Knocked out in the first round," he said. "They got me on a technical scratch." I nodded in sympathy, though I wouldn't know a technical scratch from a technical itch. The game they played was not exactly eight ball.

He frowned at the chart, trying to read it upside-down. "They really snaffed your pretty chart, sister."

"It was meant to be snaffed with," she said. "We're making up a new one."

"Call it out to everyone tonight or in the morning," I said. "Give them something to do other than shovel snow."

"Your mind's made up?" he said to Sara. "You're going to take the big jump? And when you come back, I won't even be dust anymore."

"Your choice," she said, "as well as mine."

He nodded amiably. "I mean, I can see why Mom and Dad—"

"We've had this conversation before."

I could hear the house creak. Settling under the weight of snow. Marygay was sitting silent in the kitchen, listening.

"Run it by again," I said. "Things have changed since I last heard it."

"What, that you're taking one of Man along? And a Tauran?"

"You'll be Man by then."

He looked at me for a long moment. "No."

"It shouldn't make any difference which individual goes. Group mind and all."

"Bill doesn't have the right genes," Sara said. "They'll want to send a real Man." That was a pun that saw daily use.

"I wouldn't go anyhow. It stinks of suicide."

"There's not much danger," I said. "More danger staying here, actually."

"That's true. You're less likely to die in the next ten years than I am in the next forty thousand."

I smiled. "Ten versus ten."

"It's still running away. You're bored with this life and you're deathly afraid of growing old. I'm not either of those things."

"What you *are* is twenty-one and all-knowing."

"Yeah, bullshit."

"And what you don't know is what life used to be like, without Man or Tauran to complicate things. Or make things easier, by brainwashing you."

"Brainwashing. You haven't brought that up in weeks."

"It's as obvious as a wart on your nose. But like a wart, you don't see it because you're used to it."

Bill exploded. "What I *am* used to is this constant nagging!" He stood up. "Sara, you can supply the answers. Keep talking, Dad. I'm gonna go take a nap."

"So who's running away now?"

"Just tired. Really tired."

Marygay was at the kitchen door. "Don't you want some soup?"

"Not hungry, Mom. I'll zap some later." He took the stairs two at a time.

"I do know the answers by heart," Sara said, smiling, "if you want to run through the logic again."

"You're not the one I'm losing," I said. "Even though you plan to go over to the enemy someday." She looked down at her chart and growled something in Tauran. "What does that mean?"

"It's part of their catechism. It sort of means 'Own nothing, lose nothing.' " She looked up and her eyes were bright. "It also means 'Love nothing, lose nothing.' They use the words interchangeably."

She stood up slowly. "I want to talk to him." When I went up to bed, an hour and a half later, they were still arguing in whispers.

I t was Bill's turn to fix breakfast the next morning, and he was silent as he worked over the corn cakes and eggs. I started to compliment him when he served them, but he cut me short: "I'm going. I'm going with you."

"What?"

"I've changed my mind." He looked at Sara. "Or had it changed. Sister says there's room for another guy in aquaculture."

"And you have a natural love for that," I said.

"The head-chopping part, anyhow." He sat down. "It *is* the chance of a lifetime, of many lifetimes. And I won't be that old, when we get back."

"Thank you," Marygay said, her voice wavering. Bill nodded. Sara smiled.

The next few months were tiring but interesting. We spent ten or twelve hours a week in the library's ALSC—Accelerated Life Situation Computer—learning or relearning the arcana of spaceflight. Marygay had gone through it before; everyone who went on the time shuttle had to know the basics of how the ship was run.

Unsurprisingly, things had gotten simpler in the centuries since I was last in training. One person could actually control the whole ship, under normal circumstances.

We trained for specialties, too. For me it was shuttle piloting and the suspended-animation facility, which made me long for summer even more than usual.

We were through first winter and well into deep winter before word came from Earth.

Some people like deep winter for its austere simplicity. It

rarely snows. The diminished sun climbs its same steady course. It gets down to thirty or forty below at night; sixty-five below before thaw season begins.

The people who like deep winter are not fishermen. When the lake is solid enough to walk on, I go out to make ninety-six holes in the ice, using hollow heated cylinders.

Each cylinder is a meter of thick aluminum with a heating element wound through inside. The cylinder is flared with insulation at the top so as not to sink. I set out a dozen at a time, upright, spaced evenly for the trotlines, then turn them on and wait. After a couple of hours, they melt through, and I turn off the power. Wait another hour or so, and then the fun begins.

Of course by the time the ice is refrozen on the inside, the outside is stuck fast. I carry a sledgehammer and a crowbar. I whang around the outside of the cylinder until there's a cracking, sucking sound, and then I take hold of the flange and haul this thirty-kilogram ice cube up. I turn the power on that one up high and move down to repeat the process on the next one.

By the time I get to the end of the dozen, the first one has warmed enough so that I can slip it off the bar of ice it's holding. Then I use the crowbar to break up the ice that's re-formed in the hole, slip the aluminum sleeve back in, turn the power down to minimum, cap it, and move to the next one.

The reason for this rigamarole is a combination of thermodynamics and fish psychology. I have to keep the water in the hole at exactly zero or the fish won't bite. But if you don't start out with liquid water—just melt through—you wind up with a cylinder of ice clinking around in it. The fish will bite the hook, but hang up and get away.

Bill and Sara did half the holes one day, and Marygay and I did the other half the next. When we came in from work, late afternoon, the house smelled wonderful. Sara was roasting a chicken over the fire, and had made hot mulled cider with sweet wine.

She wasn't in the kitchen. Marygay and I poured cups and went into the living room.

Our children were sitting silently with a Man. I recognized him by his bulk and the scar. "Afternoon, Sheriff."

Without preamble: "The Whole Tree said no."

I sat down heavily, sloshing some cider. Marygay sat on the couch armrest. "Just that?" she said. "Only 'no' and nothing more?"

My spinning mind came up with "Quoth the Raven, 'Nevermore.' "

"There are details." He pulled out a four- or five-page document, folded over, and set it on the coffee table.

"Basically, they thank you for your work, and have paid each of the one hundred fifty volunteers one one-hundred-fiftieth of what the ship is worth."

"In Earth credits, no doubt," I said.

"Yes . . . but also a trip to Earth, to spend it. It *is* a large fortune, and could make life easier and more interesting for all of you."

"Let all one hundred fifty of us aboard?"

"No." The sheriff smiled. "You might go someplace other than Earth."

"How many, and which of us?"

"Seventeen; you choose. They'll be in suspended animation during the flight, as a security precaution."

"While Man does the flying and life support. How many of you?"

"I wasn't told. How many would it take?"

"Maybe twenty, if ten were farmers." We hadn't actually thought in terms of minimums. "Are any of you farmers?"

"I don't know of any. We learn very fast, though."

"I suppose you do." Not the response a farmer would give.

"Have you offered the sheriff some cider?" Marygay said.

"I can't stay," he said. "I just wanted you two to hear before the general broadcast."

"That was kind," I said. "Thank you."

He stood up and began putting on layers of clothes. "Well, you have a special interest in it." He shook his head. "I was surprised. I thought the project was all gain and no real loss, which of course was the consensus here." He gestured at the table. "This was not just our Whole Tree's decision, though. It's very curious."

I ushered him out, as far as the waist-deep channel cut through the snow to the driveway. The sun was getting low and the air sucked my body heat away. Two breaths and my moustache froze into bristles.

Only two years till spring. Real years.

Marygay was almost done reading it when I came back inside. She was on the verge of tears. "What does it say?"

Without taking her eyes from the last sheet, she handed me the first three. "The Taurans. It's the god-damn Taurans."

The first couple of pages were the expected economic argument, which, with scrupulous fairness, they admitted was not reason enough by itself to deny us the time shuttle.

But their group mind hooked up with the Tauran group mind, and the Taurans said *absolutely no*. It was too dangerous—not to us, but to them.

And they couldn't explain why.

"They used to say, 'There are things man was not meant to

know.' " I looked at the kids. "That was when 'man' meant us."

"That's what this adds up to," Marygay said. "Nothing like an actual explanation." She felt along the bottom of the last sheet. "There's some Tauran here." They did official documents in a Braille-like language. "Can you read it?"

"Just simple things," Sara said. She ran a finger along the lines. "No. I'll take it to the library after school, and scan it."

"Thanks," I said. "I'm sure it'll clear everything up."

"Oh, Dad. Sometimes they're not strange at all." She got up. "Check the chicken. It should be almost done."

It was a good dinner. She had roasted potatoes and carrots in the coals, wrapped in foil with garlic butter and herbs.

The kids were animated all through dinner. Marygay and I were not good company. After dinner we watched a couple of hours of cube, an ice-skating show that made me reheat the cider.

Upstairs, getting ready for bed, she finally started to cry. Just silently wiping tears.

"I guess I should have been more ready for this. I hadn't thought about the Taurans, though. Man is usually reasonable."

We peeled back sheet, blanket, and quilt, and bundled in against the cold. "Twenty more months of this," she said.

"Not for us," I said.

"What do you mean?"

"The hell with the Taurans and their mysticism. Back to Plan A."

"Plan A?"

"We highjack the bastard."

*   *   *

Sara brought home the Tauran writing at noon. "The librarian said it was a ritual statement, like the end of a prayer: 'Inside the foreign, the unknown; inside that, the unknowable.' She said that was only close. There aren't exact human translations for the concepts."

I found a pen and had her repeat it slowly, and printed it in block letters on the back. She went into the kitchen to fix a sandwich. "Wow. What are you doing with all the stuff?"

"Nothing else scheduled till four. Thought I'd take care of everything at once." Out of an obscure impulse, I'd brought inside every farming and fishing implement that held an edge or came to a point, and was cleaning and sharpening them. They were stacked in a glittering array along the dining-room table. "Been putting it off, since it's been too cold to work in the shed."

I hadn't expected anyone to be home this early. She walked by them with a nod, though. She'd grown up around them, and didn't see them as weapons.

We had lunch together in amiable silence, surrounded by axes and gaffs, reading.

She finished her sandwich and looked straight at me. "Dad, I want to go with you."

I was startled. "What?"

"To Earth. You'll be one of the seventeen, won't you?"

"Your mother and me, yes. That was in the note. It didn't say how the other fifteen would be chosen, though."

"Maybe they'll let you choose."

"Maybe so. You'll be at the top of my list."

"Thanks, Dad." She gave me a kiss on the cheek, bundled up, and hurried back to school.

I wondered if I understood quite what had just transpired— or whether she knew, at some level. Fathers and daughters don't communicate that well even when alien languages and secret conspiracies aren't involved.

Marygay and I had been chosen, of course, since we were the only two people alive who remembered twentieth-century Earth, before the Forever War. Man would be interested in our impressions. I supposed the other fifteen were to be chosen at random, from people who wanted to make the trip—probably half the planet.

There would be no trip, of course. The ship would be accelerating straight up to nowhere. With Sara aboard, as originally planned.

I unrolled the revised loading schedule she'd prepared, weighing down the four corners with salt and pepper shakers and two wicked-looking knives.

It was discouraging, the hundreds of things that would have to be brought to the spaceport and launched into orbit. They weren't going to bother with all that, just going to Earth and back. So we'd have to highjack the *Time Warp* and then somehow keep control of the situation long enough to launch the shuttles dozens of times. The people alone would take up ten flights.

We weren't going to do it by attacking them with a bunch of farm implements. We somehow had to present a real threat. But there weren't many actual weapons on Middle Finger, and they were almost all in the hands of authorities like the sheriff.

I gathered up the tools to take outside. A weapon doesn't always look like a weapon. What did we have? Did we have *anything* that would keep them at bay for ten days, a couple of weeks, while the shuttles plied back and forth?

We could have, I suddenly realized. Maybe it was a little insane.

twelve

I t took planning and coordination—and an unexpected assist from our adversaries: the seventeen going to Earth were all from Paxton, more or less the ringleaders of the original plot. Whether they were planning to let us come *back* from Earth was open to question. It was also moot.

We had only twelve days before the supposed departure for Earth. I had sent all the others copies of the document from the One Tree, and we'd commiserated and talked about how, among other things, we might still get approval for our long journey, after talking to Man and Tauran on Earth.

While talking on the cube to them, I made a casual gesture, touching middle finger to cheekbone, that used to be phone code: "Disregard this; someone may be listening." Most of them returned the gesture.

Not one word of the plot was communicated by voice or

electronics. I wrote down brief and precise descriptions of each person's role, the notes to be memorized and destroyed. Even Marygay and I never spoke of it, not even when we were tending the trotlines, alone out on the ice.

The seventeen of us saw a lot of each other, talking about Earth and passing notes about escape. The consensus seemed to be that it probably wouldn't work, but we didn't have time to come up with anything more refined.

I wished I could have told Sara. She was disconsolate at being denied a chance for Earth; a chance to leave Middle Finger just once in her life.

I tried not to smile too much. "Do something, even if it's wrong," my mother used to say. We were finally doing something.

Middle Finger didn't have an army; just a lightly armed police force to keep order. There were very few weapons on the planet—nothing to go hunting for with anything more lethal than a hook and line.

But there was one weapon potentially more dangerous than all the small arms at Man's disposal. In the Museum of History in Centrus, there was a fighting suit left over from the Forever War.

Even stripped of its nuclear and conventional explosives, even with the laser finger deactivated, it was still a formidable weapon because of its strength-amplification circuitry and armor. (We knew the circuitry was intact because Man occasionally dusted it off for construction and demolition jobs.) A man or woman inside it became like a demigod of myth—or, for my generation, a superhero of comics. Able to leap tall buildings in a single bound. Kill a person with a single punch.

You could power up a cold suit from almost any source. It

could suck the energy out of a floater and have enough juice for a little mayhem—or a couple of hours' searching for a better source.

We couldn't assume the suit was powered up, sitting there waiting to be taken—though Charlie argued that it probably was, for the same reason there was no military force in Centrus to keep us in line. If we fought Man and won, what would we accomplish, from their point of view? They saw themselves as mentors and partners, our conduit to true civilization. There was no need for Man to take precautions against a useless and futile action.

We were to learn otherwise.

Max Weston was the only person I knew who was physically large and strong enough that I had no doubt he could overpower the sheriff. We needed his weapons in order to attack the museum. We had to take them at the last minute, of course, just before we left for Centrus. We could lock him up in his own cell or possibly take him hostage. (I argued against killing him, or anyone, if we could help it. Max agreed too easily, I thought.)

Our timetable was set by Man. An express floater would arrive at noon on 10 Copernicus, and an hour later we would be in Centrus. We were to spend the afternoon in a last-minute briefing, then be prepped for suspended animation and shuttled up to the *Time Warp* as part of the baggage.

Max raised the possibility, which had occurred to me and probably others, that they had no intention of prepping us for SA. They would give us a shot not to suspend our animation, but to end it. Send the *Time Warp* off and have it come back without us, with some sad story—we all died of a rare Earth disease, because of lack of immunity—and MF would somehow have to get along without seventeen troublemakers.

It sounded paranoiac; I doubted that Man saw us as a threat worth disposing of, and if indeed they did, there were less elaborate ways to go about doing it. But then Man often did things in elaborate and unlikely ways. Comes from hanging around with Taurans all the time, I guess.

Our timing had to be precise, and a lot of machines had to work. The sheriff's weapons would get us the fighting suit; the fighting suit would get us the shuttle, and the shuttle would take us to the ultimate weapon.

But the plan would stop dead if, for instance, the sheriff's weapons were programmed to work only for him—they had that technology more than a millennium ago—or if the fighting suit wouldn't crank, or if the shuttle or the *Time Warp* had an override that could be controlled from the ground. In our ALSC training as pilots, me for the shuttle and Marygay for the starship, there was nothing about that; both vehicles were autonomous systems. It was possible they had withheld a few details from our training, though.

We were careful not to arrive at the town hall all at once. It did simplify our operation that the floater was picking us up right at the sheriff's door, and we probably could have all come down as a group. But the plan was for Marygay and me to come early and distract the sheriff, and be there to help Max, if necessary.

Bill and Sara drove us down at eleven o'clock with our small bag—toiletries and a few changes of clothing and two long knives. We hadn't told them anything. Bill was in a good mood, negotiating the icy streets with smooth speed. Sara was subdued, maybe holding back tears. She really had wanted to come, and probably thought we hadn't worked hard enough to get her added to the list.

"We should tell them," Marygay said as we pulled up to the police station.

"Tell what?" Sara said.

"You're not missing any trip to Earth," I said. "We're not going to Earth. We've gone back to the original plan."

"We'll all be on the *Time Warp* in a couple of weeks," Marygay said, "headed for the future, not the past."

"I hadn't heard," Bill said slowly. "You'd think they would've said something about it."

"They don't know about it yet. The sheriff's about to find out."

Bill set the brake and turned around in the driver's seat. "You're going to take it by force?"

"In a way," Marygay said. "If things go according to plan, nobody will be hurt."

"Can I help? I'm bigger than you."

"Not now." Glad he asked, though. "It has to look like things are going according to *their* plan, until we get to Centrus."

"Just act as if nothing were different, darlings. Keep an eye on the news."

"Don't . . ." Sara said. "Don't get . . . don't do, don't take any chances?"

"We'll be careful," Marygay said. Sara was probably trying to say *Don't do anything foolish*, but I'm afraid we'd moved beyond that stage.

I kissed them both and opened the door. Marygay kissed them and held on to Bill for an extra second. "See you soon."

"Good luck," Bill said urgently. Sara nodded, biting her lower lip. I closed the door behind Marygay and they were gone.

"Well," I said pointlessly, "here we go." She nodded and we picked our way up the icy steps and pushed through the double doors.

The sheriff wasn't in his office; he was straightening up the reception hall. He checked his watch. "You're early."

"Bill dropped us off," Marygay said. "He had to go on to school."

He nodded. "Tea in the office."

Marygay went for tea and I went down the corridor to the toilet, mainly to check the cells. Both were open, and could be locked on the outside with a simple mechanical bolt. We'd want to take the keyboard out before we locked him in. It hadn't worked for me, but maybe I hadn't had the right combination.

I joined Marygay for tea. She glanced toward the empty peg behind the sheriff's desk. He was probably wearing the pistol under his vest, as he had the night he came to arrest us.

The door opened and we heard him greet Max. I walked into the room and saw that they were shaking hands. Max knew about the concealed holster.

My move was pretty obvious, and in retrospect I suppose it wouldn't have worked if the sheriff had been on guard. I faked tripping on the rug and dropped the mug of tea. Cried out, "Oh, shit!"

As the sheriff turned, Max clamped his forearm around his neck and grabbed his right arm. The sheriff tried to kick back, but Max had anticipated the move and blocked it; meanwhile, I reached into the sheriff's vest and yanked out the pistol.

"Don't choke him, Max!" Max dropped his left arm enough to let him breathe, at the same time forcing him to his knees.

The sheriff coughed twice. "What is this?"

"Figure it out," Max said. "Use your group mind."

Marygay came out of the office holding a big roll of building tape. "Into the cell! William . . . point the gun *at* him!"

I was holding it loosely, aimed at the floor. Might go off. I gestured with it. "Keep ahold of him, Max."

He didn't resist. "You're going to be in real trouble. Whatever you think you're doing."

"You've got that right," I said. "Real trouble now. But by the time we get back, it won't make any difference."

Max had walked him into the first cell, and pushed him down into the chair. "What? You think you can . . . you're going to take the starship?"

"These guys are fast," Max said. Marygay secured him to the chair with the tape.

"We don't mean you any harm, Sheriff," I said, "nor anyone in Centrus. We're just going ahead with what we proposed—with what you approved of."

He was regaining some composure. "But that was provisional. Before we heard from the Whole Tree."

"You do what you want," Marygay said. "We don't have to take orders from Earth."

"From *Taurans* on Earth," Max said.

"But it's not practical," the sheriff said with an edge of exasperation. "The three of you—"

"Seventeen," I said.

"Even seventeen, you can't steal the starship and run it."

"We have a plan. Just sit back and watch us."

A few people had come in and were standing at the door. "You don't seem to need any help," Jynn said.

"Look around and see if you can find any more weapons," Max said.

"There aren't any," the sheriff said, nodding at me. "Just the pistol. Just for emergencies."

"Like this." Max stuck his hand out and I gave him the pistol. He aimed it at the viewscreen over the keyboard and fired. The explosion was loud in the small room. I shielded my eyes and didn't see what it looked like, but the result was pretty dramatic. There was more hole than viewscreen.

"What the hell was that?" somebody shouted.

"Testing." He handed it back. "Works."

"You aren't going to steal the starship with an old pistol."

"We really just have to steal a shuttle," Marygay said. "The starship will do what I tell it to."

"And we'll have more than a pistol," Max said.

Cat came to the door. She and Marygay exchanged nods. "We found some crowd-control stuff. Gas grenades and tanglefoot."

"Probably what they'll use on us, in Centrus," I said. "Might as well have our own."

"The mask would be more useful," the sheriff said.

"What?"

"The gas mask. It's in the top right-hand drawer of my desk." He shrugged. "Might as well cooperate."

"We couldn't get that one open," Cat said. "Thumbprint?"

He nodded. "That's where the ammunition is, too." He wiggled his thumb. "You could bring the desk here, or set me free."

"It's a trap," Max said. "It probably sends a signal."

"Do as you wish," the Man said.

"Why would you want to help us?" Marygay said.

"For one thing, I'm on your side; I've known you since I was a boy, and know how much this means." He looked at Max. "Also, you have the gun. At least one of you could use it."

Max pulled out a big pocket knife and the blade snapped out. "I could cut off your thumb." He sawed at the tape and freed him. "Move slowly, now."

The drawer had the ammo and gas mask, and also handcuffs and ankle restraints. We put them on the sheriff.

"Floater's here," Po said from the door.

"Driver?" Marygay called back. He said no; it had the au-
todriver light on. "You're coming along, then. Hostage."

"If you leave me locked up in the cell, there's no way I could
hamper you. I'd prefer that."

Max grabbed his arm. "We'd prefer to have you along."

"Wait," I said. "You think they're going to kill us."

"As soon as they see you're armed, yes. My being with you
wouldn't affect the decision."

"One reason we love you so much," Marygay said. "Your
concern for one another."

"It wouldn't just be Man making that decision," he said; "not
in Centrus. A Tauran truly wouldn't understand why it made any
difference."

"They let Taurans in on police matters?"

"No, but it won't be a police thing, once the starship's part
of it. Matters that involve space are going to involve Taurans."

"The more reason for a hostage," Max said.

"Do you hear yourself?" the sheriff said. "Which of us now
is placing a low value on life?"

"Just on yours," Max said, and gave him a push toward the
door.

"Wait," I said. "Until they know what we're doing, there
won't be any Taurans involved?"

"Only people and Man," he said. "But it won't take them
long to see what's happening and contact the Taurans."

"Yeah." I pointed at the door. "Take him out and lock him
up. We have to confer."

Max was back in a minute. "It may be time to gamble," I
said. "The floater's going to go down Main to get to the spaceport. I could slip out by the museum, and you all go on. With

the sheriff, you'll have the expected seventeen people, if any-body's looking. That will gain us some time. Then you can dis-able the floater before it gets there."

"But then you don't have the floater's fuel cell." We had planned on that in case the fighting suit was cold.

"Yes, he will," Max said, intense. "We get a klick or so from the spaceport and put the floater on manual and ground it. That's five, maye seven minutes from dropping him off. Give him a minute or two to get into trouble. Then we turn the floater around and take it back to him."

"With the police in hot pursuit," Marygay said.

"Maybe; maybe not," I said. "You keep the gun, in case, but hell. They don't *have* police like on Earth." Probably not on Earth now, either. "Unarmed traffic cops."

"You don't want the gun?" Max said.

"No—look; that tear gas is a godsend. I go in with the tear gas and the mask and a crowbar, I'll be inside the suit in minutes. Hell, I'll meet you on the road to the spaceport."

Marygay nodded. "It could work. And if it doesn't, at least you won't have used a deadly weapon on the guard."

I was able to stuff the gas grenades and mask into the sher-iff's briefcase. Hard to disguise a crowbar, but I found I could slide it down my pants leg to the knee, and the belt held it in place, with the top part concealed by my coat.

We all got situated in the floater and it took off, rising to about a hundred meters. The snow had gotten pretty heavy; you couldn't see the ground. We hoped it was like this in Centrus. It would slow things down for them, but not for us, so long as the wind stayed calm. The shuttle was okay in snow but wouldn't launch in a strong crosswind.

It was an uncomfortable hour. The sheriff wasn't the only

hostage, in fact; everyone else's fate was dependent on the outcome of a string of unpredictable events. And nobody wanted to talk about it, not with the sheriff listening.

I became curiously calm as the floater dropped to ground level, near the city limits. There was a certain amount of danger ahead, but it was thin soup compared to what I remembered of combat.

I didn't want to think about how many years ago that was. I hoped the museum guards were soft city boys and girls—bookish and unfamiliar with violence. Maybe old folks. I'd give them a story for the grandkids, regardless. "I was there when the crazy vets highjacked the starship." Or maybe "One day this crazy guy ran in with tear gas. I shot him." But none of us could remember the museum guards being armed, which *would* have been memorable. Maybe they just kept the guns out of sight. Maybe I should worry about something else.

Marygay had her thumb on the OVERRIDE button, but it wasn't necessary. The floater stopped for cross-traffic a block before the library. I gave her a kiss and slipped out the door.

The snow was sifting down slowly, straight—still good for the shuttle and perhaps for me, since it would slow down response to a call for help from the museum. I threaded my way through the inching traffic, people perhaps being extra-courteous because of my limp. The crowbar had slid past my knee.

It occurred to me that the museum might be closed, and that might be a good thing. I could break in and, although it would doubtless set off an alarm, I would just be dealing with police, and not a lot of bystanders.

No such luck. As I approached the museum, someone was leaving, backing out the front door with a wide covered tray, probably breakfast.

I went through the heavy wooden door, and sure enough, the guard was nibbling at a piece of cake from a stack of assorted kinds on a plate. She was a female Man, in her early twenties. She said something to me in their language, mumbling through a mouthful. I think she said good morning, and invited me to leave my coat and attaché case there.

She had the broad chin they all have, a good target for a punch. When she looked inside the case, I'd give her an upper-cut that I hoped would knock her out for a minute and leave her disorganized for another.

It wasn't necessary. She asked me what was in the bag, and I said, in slow English, "I don't know. I'm from Paxton, supposed to deliver this to the Man in charge of the weapons exhibit."

"Oh, he's not a Man; he's one of you. Jacob Kellman, he came in two or three minutes ago. You could take it right to him, A4." The small building only had two stories, with four rooms each.

The door to A4 was closed. I opened it and there was no one inside. No lock. I eased it shut and worked fast—pulled out the crowbar and ran past all of the less potent examples of man's inhumanity to all species, straight to the glass case with the fight-ing suit. Two swings with the crowbar and the front pane of glass cascaded in.

I ran back toward the door and got there just as it opened. Kellman was a greybeard, at least as old as me, unarmed. Draw-ing on my vast knowledge of hand-to-hand combat, I shoved him hard and he fell down sprawling in the corridor. I slammed the door shut again and wedged the crowbar in between the door and the jamb, as a crude lock, and hurried back to the exhibit.

The fighting suit was a newer model than the last one I'd had, but I hoped the basic design hadn't changed. I reached into the concealed niche between the shoulders and felt the emergency lever and pulled. It wouldn't work if there was anyone alive in the suit, but fortunately it was unoccupied. The suit clamshelled open, smashing another pane of glass, and the reassuring hydraulic wheeze meant it had power.

Someone was pounding on the door and yelling. I got one boot off and with a stockinged foot swept away enough broken glass so I could stand barefooted while I undressed. Got my sweater and pants off and tried to rip open the shirt, but the buttons were sewn on too well. While I fumbled with them, the pounding became a rhythmic heavy thump—someone bigger than Kellman was applying a shoulder to the door.

I got both gas grenades out of the briefcase, pulled the pins, and hurled them the length of the room. They popped with a satisfying swirl of opaque cloud and I stepped backward into the suit, slid my arms into the sleeves, and clenched both hands, for the "activate" signal. I didn't bother with the plumbing; I'd either hold it in or live with the results.

For a long second, nothing happened. I smelled the first acrid hint of the tear gas. Then the suit closed around me with a disconcerting jerkiness.

The monitor and displays came up and I looked to the lower left: power was at 0.05, weapons systems all dark, as expected.

A twentieth of normal power still made me a Goliath, at least temporarily. The cool machine-oil smell meant I had my own air. I reached down to pick up my clothes and fell on my face with a huge crash.

Well, it had been a long time since I'd been in one of these, and even longer since I'd used a GP unit—General Purpose, one size fits everybody. Normally, I'd had one tailored to my dimensions.

I managed to clamber back up to my feet and stuff the clothes, minus boots, into a front "pocket," just before they beat the door open. There was a lot of coughing and sneezing. One figure came staggering out of the cloud, a female Man who was pumped up like our sheriff, in a similar uniform, also with a pistol. She was holding it in both hands, waving it in my general direction, but her eyes were streaming and I assumed she hadn't seen me yet.

These people were not my concern. There was an emergency exit door behind me. I turned, rocking like a zombie from a 1950s movie, and lurched toward it. The Man fired three shots. One of them put a nice hole in a display of nuclear weapons and one broke an overhead lamp. The third must have ricocheted off my back; I heard it sing away but of course felt nothing.

I supposed she knew the suit was unarmed but extremely dangerous. I wondered how brave she would have been if I'd turned around and started lumbering toward her. But there was no time for play.

I pushed on the emergency door and it ripped open, then ducked slightly as I passed through. The suit was almost eight feet tall; not really for indoor wear.

People scattered in all directions, making considerable noise. The Man or someone else was shooting at me—an easy target, a matte-black giant in a snowscape. Twisting the wrist control turned me camo green, then sand yellow, then I finally found a glossy white surface.

I walked as fast as I could to Main, almost slipping twice in the snow. Come on, I thought, you've operated these things on frozen portal planets a few degrees above absolute zero. But not lately.

At least Main Street had salt and sand, so I could run. Some of the traffic was on manual, and it noisily parted for me as I sprinted down the middle. A lot of them went spinning dangerously out of control. I shifted back to green, so they'd have more warning.

I picked up the pace as I became more sure of the clumsy thing's abilities and limitations. I was loping along at about twenty miles per hour when I met Marygay's bus, just outside the city limits.

She opened the driver's-side door and stepped halfway out. "Do you need power?" she shouted.

"Not yet." The readout said 0.04. "Back at the spaceport."

She spun it on its axis and slid to the outbound lane, sending a delivery van that was on auto straight out into a field of snow. The people on manual were all pulling over, evidently from some police command; it was interesting that the ones on auto took longer to comply.

They were no doubt clearing traffic to get to me. I ran after Marygay as fast as I could, but soon lost her in the white distance.

What could they send after a fighting suit? I'd find out soon enough.

Strident blue flashing lights cut throught the swirling snow as I approached the spaceport. Marygay's bus was blocked at the entrance by a Security floater.

Two officers, evidently unarmed, were standing by the driver's side, yelling at her. She looked down on them pleasantly, and gave no reaction when I passed behind them.

I picked up one end of the Security floater and easily flipped it over. It went crashing down into a drainage ditch. The two officers, sensibly, ran like hell.

The lack of radio contact was a handicap. I bent down next

to her window. "Park it up by the main building and I'll drain the fuel cell there."

She said okay and sped off. My power was down to 0.01 and the numerals started flashing red. That would be great, stranded a couple of hundred meters from my destination. Well, I could always open the suit manually. And run naked through the snow.

As soon as I started walking, the suit added a "beep . . . beep" in time with the flashing digits, I suppose as a convenience for the blind. The legs started to resist my commands, feeling as if I were walking through water, and then mud.

I did make it to the floater while the people were still unloading. Max stood there with his arms crossed, the pistol prominent.

I popped the rear utility door and clipped my emergency cables to the fuel cell's terminals, and studied the directions on the grimy plate on the side of the cell. Then I pushed the "fast discharge" button and watched my numbers start to climb.

They'd reached 0.24 when I heard the heavy thrum of a floater braking, and found out what they could send after a fighting suit.

Two fighting suits. One human; one Tauran.

If they were armed, I was nothing but a target. Either suit's weapons could vaporize me or slice me like lunchmeat. But they didn't fire, or couldn't.

The floater lurched as the Man got out, and he repeated my performance, falling on his face. I resisted the impulse to tell him that the longest journey begins with a single step.

In the floater, the Tauran suit flailed, trying to keep its balance, and tipped over backwards. Neither of them had any more recent practice than I had. My hundreds of hours of training and fighting, even though mostly lost in the mists of time, might be worth more than their two-to-one advantage.

The Man had gotten up on hands and knees; I covered the distance with a graceless leap and swiveled a hard side-kick to the head. It probably didn't hurt him physically, but it sent the suit skidding and tumbling.

I grabbed the front bumper of the floater, my strength amplification whining loud, and tried to swing the heavy machine around to bash the Tauran. It managed to dodge, and the effort made me stagger and fall. The floater buzzed away like an angry insect.

The Tauran threw itself on me, but I kicked it away. I was trying to resurrect what I once knew about Tauran fighting suits; what weakness might give me an advantage, but all the musty ALSC stuff was about weapon systems, range, and response speed, which unfortunately seemed not to apply.

And then the Man was on me, falling on my shoulders with a crash like some heavy playground bully. He tried to grab my suit's head, and I batted his hands away—that was a good target; the suit's brain wasn't in the head, but its eyes and ears were.

I flipped him away clumsily. My weapons systems' telltales were still dark, but I tried the laser finger on him anyhow. When it didn't lance out and cut into his suit, I was curiously relieved. My underdeveloped killer instinct hadn't become fiercer with age.

While I was peering through the snow for something I could use as a weapon, the Tauran had found one; it whacked me from behind, across the shoulders, with an uprooted light pole. I went down and plowed into a snowbank. While I staggered up, it kept clanging against my shoulders and upraised arms.

My visual sensors were smeared, but I could see well enough to aim a kick between its legs, an aim more anthropomorphic than practical—but it did unbalance the thing enough for me to grab hold of the light post and jerk it away. I had seen the Man in my peripheral vision, running toward me; I swung the pole around in a flat arc and caught him at knee level. He spun sideways and hit the ground hard.

I turned to face the Tauran again, but couldn't see it, which didn't mean it was far away or hidden—all three of us were white lost in white, invisible from fifty meters in the rolling snow. I tongued over to infrared, which might work if it turned its back to me, with the heat exchangers. That didn't work and neither did radar, which I expected to work only if the suit moved in front of a reflecting surface.

I turned back to see the Man lying there motionless. Maybe a trick, or maybe I actually had knocked him out when I knocked him down. The head's protected with padding, but force is force, and he might have slammed into the ground hard enough to sustain a concussion. I feinted at him, a kick that missed his head by a hair, and he didn't react.

Where the hell was the Tauran? No sign in any direction. I crouched to pick up the Man and heard, from the direction of the spaceport, a woman's scream, muffled by the snow, then two shots.

I ran toward it, but was a moment too late. The floater was rising fast, slanting away from the smashed front entrance; Max was standing with the pistol aimed at the machine, but with no useful target. I jumped with all my amplified might, and went up maybe twenty meters, almost high enough to touch it, and then fell back down with a crash that rattled my teeth and made my ankles sting.

"The thing got Jynn," Max said. "It dove through the glass and snatched her and Roberta." Roberta was sitting in the snow, cradling her elbow.

"You all right?" They both flinched; I realized I'd inadvertently cranked up the sound. I chinned it down.

"Damn near yanked my arm off. But I'm okay."

"Where is everybody?"

"We split up," Max said. "Marygay went on with the bus, out to the shuttle. We stayed here with the gun, try to distract them."

"Well, you did that." I hesitated. "Nothing we can do here now. Let's go catch the bus." I scooped up Roberta, then Max, and stepped out on the field, carrying them like bundles. The bus wasn't visible, but it had blown a clear path through the snow. We caught up with them in less than a minute, and my passengers seemed happy to switch conveyances.

No sign of the floater with the Tauran and Jynn. I could have heard it if it were within a couple of klicks.

The bus was crowded. There were two humans I didn't recognize, and four Men, evidently our welcoming committee.

"They've got Jynn," I told Marygay. "The Taurans took her off on their floater."

She shook her head. "Jynn?" They were pretty close.

"There's nothing we can do. She's just gone."

"They won't hurt her," Max said. "Let's move!"

"Right," Marygay said, but she didn't move.

"I'll meet you at the shuttle," I said. I was too big and heavy for the bus.

"Meet you there," she said quietly, and pushed the button that closed the door. The bus lurched forward and I jogged past it toward the shuttle launch tube.

I tapped the tube elevator door button and it opened, looking warm in its yellow light. Then I popped the suit and gingerly stepped out into the snow. The front pocket resisted my efforts, but after one broken thumbnail I got my clothes free and quickly pulled them on in the shelter of the elevator car.

The bus eased down by my empty open suit and I silently urged them to hurry, hurry—how long would it take for someone to just turn off the power and leave us with a useless elevator? The shuttle might be autonomous, but we did have to get inside it to use it.

Marygay spent a few precious seconds telling the four Men and two humans to get out of here and underground, which they probably knew. The launch tube would absorb the gamma rays for the first seconds of launch, but after that it would not be wise to be nearby. Roberta had her thumb on the up button and mashed it as soon as Marygay sprinted inside.

Nobody pulled the plug. The elevator surged up and clicked into place alongside the shuttle airlock, which irised open.

Getting seated was not simple, gravity against us. We climbed down a ladder net and filled the compartment from the bottom up. The sheriff's hands and feet were freed for the job and he didn't resist being taped into place again, once he was belted in.

I settled into the pilot's seat and started snapping the sequence of switches that would get us out of here. It wasn't complicated, since there were only four standard orbit choices. I chose "Rendezvous with *Time Warp*," and had to more or less trust the ship.

The viewscreen came on and it was Jynn. The focus pulled back to show that she was in a floater, next to a Tauran.

The Tauran pointed to the windows next to Jynn. Vague through the snow, you could just make out the twin shuttle launch towers.

"Please proceed," the Tauran said. "Three seconds after you launch, this woman and I will be killed by your radiation."

"Do it," Jynn said. "Just go."

"I don't think you will," the Tauran said. "That would be inhuman. Murder in cold blood."

Marygay was next to me, in the copilot seat. "Jynn—" she started.

"You don't have any choice," Jynn said evenly. "For the next part to work, you have to show . . . what you're willing to do."

We looked at each other, both frozen.

"Do what she says," Max whispered.

Suddenly, Jynn's elbow jabbed out and drove into the Tauran's throat. Her wrists were bound with metal handcuffs; she twisted them around its neck and jerked sideways with a loud *crack*.

She pulled the inert creature down across her lap and reached sideways for the floater controls. It whined and her image bobbed. "Give me thirty seconds," she shouted over the straining motor. "No, twenty—I'll be behind the main building. Get the hell out of here!"

"You come here!" Marygay said. "We can wait!"

Maybe she didn't hear. But she didn't answer, and her image disappeared.

In her place, the calm image of a male Man in a grey tunic. "If you attempt to launch, we will shoot you down. Don't waste your lives and our shuttle."

"Even if you could do it," I said, "you probably wouldn't." I checked my watch; I'd give her the full thirty seconds. "You don't have any anti-spacecraft or anti-aircraft weapons here."

"We have them in orbit," he said. "You will all die."

"Bullshit," I said, and turned half around to face the others. "He's bluffing. Stalling for time."

Po's face was ashen. "Even if he is not. We've come this far. Let's finish it."

"That's right," Teresa said. "Whatever happens."

Thirty seconds. "Hold on." I slammed the FIRE switch down.

There was a tremendous roar and the gee force went from one to three in the short time it took us to clear the launch tube. Snow streamed away from the front viewport and was suddenly gone, replaced with bright sunshine.

The shuttle rolled over for orbital insertion, and the solid-looking clouds of the storm drifted away. The sky darkened from cobalt to indigo.

They might well have weapons in orbit, I knew. Even if they were antiques left over from the Forever War, they could do the job.

But there was absolutely nothing I could do to affect that. No evasive maneuvers or counterattacks or even clever arguments. A kind of tentative and temporary calmness settled over me, that I remembered from combat: you may only be alive for the next few seconds, but whatever happens, it will just happen. I carefully tilted my head against the acceleration and could see the strained half-smile on Marygay's face; she was in the same state.

Then the sky turned black, and we were still alive. The roar abated and then was silent. We floated through space in free fall.

I looked back. "Everybody okay?" They murmured tentative assent, though some of them looked pretty bad. The anti-nausea medicine worked for most people, but of course space travel wasn't the only stress they were going through.

We watched the *Time Warp* grow from brightest star to non-stellar sparkle to a hard bright image that grew and then loomed. The automated part of our trip ended with a not-quite-human voice telling me that control would be surrendered to me in ten seconds . . . nine . . . and so forth.

Actually, it was responsibility rather than "control" that had been transferred to me; the shuttle's radar still mediated the rate of approach to the docking area. I kept my right hand gripped on a dead-man's switch; if anything seemed wrong, I would let go, and the previous moment's maneuvers would be quickly reversed.

The airlocks mated with a reassuring metallic snap, and my ears popped as our air pressure dropped to match the thin but oxygen-rich mixture in the *Time Warp*.

"Phase Two," I said. "Let's go see whether it works."

"I think it will work," the sheriff said. "You've done the hard part."

I looked at him. "There's no way you could have learned our plans. *No* way."

"That's right."

"But you know us so well—you're so superior—that you knew exactly what we were going to do."

"I would not put it so harshly. But yes, I was told to expect rebellion and perhaps violence, and advised not to resist."

"And the rest of it? What we're about to do?"

"That's a mystery to me, or conjecture; I was asked not to tap the Whole Tree, so I wouldn't know too much."

"But the others know. Or think they know."

"I've said too much. Just continue with what you're doing. You may learn from it."

"*You* may learn something," Max said.

"Let's move along," Marygay said. "Whatever they've got set up for us, whatever they think they know, it doesn't change Phase Two."

"You're wrong," Max said. "We should find out what we can from this bastard. We can't lose anything by squeezing him."

"Or gain anything," the sheriff said. "I've told you all I know."

"Let's find out," Roberta said. "Max is right. Nothing to lose."

"A lot to lose," I said. "You sound like my old drill sergeants. This is a negotiation, not a war."

"They were threatening to kill us," Po said. "If it's not a war, it's something close to it."

Marygay came to my rescue. "Leave it as an option. Right now, I think we're ahead for not having hurt or coerced him."

"Other than beating him up and tying him down," Roberta said.

"If we ultimately have to force information out of him," Marygay pushed on, "then we can do it. Right now we have to act, not talk." She rubbed her face. "Besides, they probably have their own hostage by now. Jynn couldn't get far in that floater."

"Jynn killed one of them," Max said. "She's dead meat."

"You shut up, Max."

"If she's alive, she's a liability."

"Shut up."

"You home cunts," Max said. "You always—"

"My wife is not a cunt or a home." I tried to keep my voice down. "When we walk through that door she'll be your commander."

"And I have no problem with that. I had a long career and never saw a het commander. But if you think *she's* het, you're blind as a worm."

"Max," Marygay said quietly, "my *heart* has been het and home and irrelevant, as now. William is in charge on this ship, and you're being insubordinate."

"You're right," he said flatly. To me: "I lost my head and I apologize. Too much has happened, too fast. And I haven't been a soldier since before my kids were born."

"Me neither," I said, and didn't push it. "Let's just move."

On the other side of the airlock, we expected it to be dark and cool, the minimum-energy mode we'd last left it in. But the artificial sun was bright and the air was warm and fragrant with growing things.

And there was a Tauran waiting for us on the shipside landing, unarmed. It made their sign of greeting, hugging itself. "You know me," it said. "Antres 906. Are you the leader, William Mandella?"

I looked beyond it to the well-tended fields. "What the hell is this?"

"I speak right now only to the leader. Are you he?"

"No." I put my hand on Marygay's shoulder. She was also staring, stunned. "My wife."

"Marygay Potter. Come with me to the control room."

"They're ready to ride," Max said behind me. "Straight to Earth." They'd told us there would be several weeks of tending to the life-support farms, before we went into suspended animation. This looked like we were headed straight to the tanks.

"How many are here, Antres?" Marygay said.

"No one else."

"This took a lot of people."

"Come with me." She followed Antres to the lift, and I came along, both of us struggling with the zerogee nets. Antres was deft with them, but elaborately slow.

We went up to the command level and picked our way into the control room. The center screen was lit, with the image of an older male Man, perhaps one we had talked to in Centrus.

Marygay climbed into the captain's chair and strapped herself in.

"Are there any further casualties?" the Man said without preamble.

"I was going to ask the same thing. Jynn Silver."

"The one who killed one of us."

"A Tauran is not 'one of us' if you are human. Is she alive?"

"Alive and in custody. I think we have deduced much of your plan. Would you care to reveal it now?"

Marygay looked at me and I shrugged.

She spoke slowly and quietly. "Our plan is that this ship is not going to Earth. We demand to be allowed to use the *Time Warp* as we originally requested."

"You can't do that without our cooperation. Forty shuttle flights. What will you do if we refuse?"

She swallowed. "We'll send everybody back on the shuttle we have. Then my husband and I will ride the *Time Warp* to the ground. Crash-land near the southern pole."

"So you think we will give you the ship rather than let you kill yourselves?"

"Well, it won't be too comfortable for you, either. When the antimatter fuel explodes, the resulting vapor will blanket Middle Finger in clouds. There will be no spring or summer, this year or next."

"The third year," I said from behind her, "will be blizzard and then floods."

"We can't allow that to happen," he said. "So all right. We accede to your demands."

We looked at each other. "That's it?"

"You give us no choice." Two data screens lit up. "The launch schedule you see here was adapted from your original timetable."

"So this is all according to plan," Marygay said. "Your plan."

"A contingency," he said, "in case you allowed us no alternative."

She laughed. "You couldn't just let us go."

"Of course not. The Whole Tree forbade that."

"Hold it," I said. "You're disobeying the Whole Tree?"

"Not at all. It is *you* who are defying it. We are only taking a reasonable course of action. *Reaction*, to your declaration of intent to wholesale murder."

"And the Whole Tree predicted this would happen?"

"Oh, no." For the first time, he allowed himself a small smile. "Men on Earth don't know you as well as we who grew up with you."

The sheriff tried to explain what he knew or could deduce about the rationale for their plan. It was like a theological argument in somebody else's religion.

"The Whole Tree is not infallible," he said. "It represents a huge and well-informed consensus. In this case, though, it was . . . it was like a thousand people taking a vote, where only two or three were *actually* well-informed."

We were all at a big table in the dining hall, drinking bad tea made from concentrate. "That's what I don't understand," Charlie said. "It seems to me that would happen more often than not." He was directly across from the sheriff, staring intently, his chin in his palm.

"No, this was a special case." He shifted uncomfortably. "Men on Earth think they know humans. They live and work with them all their lives. But they're not at all the same kind of people as you are.

"They or their ancestors chose to come to Earth, even though it meant becoming part of a small minority, outside of Man's mainstream culture."

"Trading independence for comfort," I said. "The illusion of independence."

"It's not that simple. They live more comfortably than you— or we—do, but what's more important is that they deeply wanted to come *home*. People who chose Middle Finger turned their backs on home.

"So when a Man on Earth thinks about humans, there's a profoundly different composite picture. If you took one hundred fifty Earth humans and shot them forty thousand years into the future . . . it would be cruel. Like snatching a child from its parents, and abandoning it in a foreign land."

"That's nice," Charlie said. "The Whole Tree's decision was based on concern for our happiness."

"Concern for your sanity," the sheriff said.

"The huge expense of the enterprise wasn't a factor."

"Not a large one." He made a circular gesture, indicating everything around us. "This ship represents a lot of wealth in terms of our economy. But it's not worth much in Earth terms. There are thousands of them sitting empty, parked in orbit around the Sun. This wouldn't be a big project if people on Earth had proposed it."

"But they never would," I said. "They're stay-at-homes."

He shrugged. "How many people on Middle Finger think you're crazy?"

"More than half, I guess." We only had 1,600 volunteers out of 30,000 people. "The younger half of my family does."

He nodded slowly. "But weren't they going along?"

"Bill, especially, in spite of thinking we're crazy."

"I understand that," he said. "So am I."

"What?"

"We asked that you take a Man and a Tauran."

The Tauran spoke up for the first time. "We are they," it growled.

book three

THE BOOK OF
EXODUS

thirteen

The timetable had called for fifteen days' loading before launch, but that presupposed everybody being packed and waiting. Instead, they'd had two weeks to rearrange their lives, knowing that the expedition had been scotched.

We lost 12 out of the original 150. Replacing them was not as simple as asking for volunteers, since they'd been chosen with an eye toward a certain demographic mix and assortment of skills.

Forty thousand years from now, we might come back to an unpopulated planet. We wanted our descendants to have a chance at civilization.

We didn't have unlimited leisure for revision, juggling the shuttle schedule while we found replacements. Word had of course gone to Earth about our insurrection, so ten months from now there might be some response. If they had thousands of ships at their disposal, a few of them might be faster than the *Time Warp*; a lot faster.

A hundred fifty people were sufficient for a town-hall kind of democracy. We'd worked out the structure a couple of months before. There was an elected Council of five, each one of whom would serve a year as mayor, and then retire, a new councilor being elected each year.

So we worked as fast as we could, without cutting corners. Fortunately, none of the elected officials were among the ones who decided to stay home, so our little bureaucracy was intact. We probably had to make more decisions in a couple of weeks than we would in two years aboard the ship.

But it was a ship as well as a town, and the ship's captain had authority over the mayor and council. Both Marygay and I were nominated for captain, along with Anita Szydhowska, who had been with me in the Sade-138 campaign. Anita stepped down in favor of us, and I stepped down in favor of Marygay, and no one objected. Both Anita and I were elected councilors. The other three were Chance Delany, Stephen Funk, and Sage Ten. Diana Alsever-Moore was nominated but declined, arguing that as the ship's only doctor, she wouldn't have time for a hobby.

It only took twenty days to get everyone aboard the ship. I wondered whether anyone else, watching the shuttles leave for the last time, had the image—old-fashioned even in my youth—of the last ropes being thrown back onto the dock, as a great ship left its safe harbor.

The last shuttle was supposed to have our children aboard. It was one short. Sara floated over to us and wordlessly handed me a sheet of paper.

I love you but I never did intend to come with you. Sara talked me into pretending that I would, so that we would stop wasting time fighting. It was dishonest but I think I agree it was the best thing.

I'm somewhere in Centrus. Don't try to find me.

If I was not loyal to you I could have stopped the whole thing the day we left you at the sheriff's. But I guess we all have to be crazy in our own way.

Have a good 40,000 years.

Love, Bill

The blood had drained from Marygay's face. I handed her the note, but of course she knew what was in it.

I felt loss, but also a strange relief. And I wasn't completely surprised; at some level I guess I'd known something was going on.

Maybe Marygay had, too. She stared at the note and then slipped it under the other sheets on her clipboard, cleared her throat, and spoke to the new arrivals with only a slight quaver in her voice. "These are your initial housing assignments. We'll be trading around. But put your stuff in there now, and come back to the assembly area. Is anybody feeling space-sick?"

One big man obviously was; his skin had a greenish cast. He raised his hand. "I'll take you to the doctor," I said. "She has something stronger than that pill." He actually made it to the clinic before he barfed.

There were ten communication channels, and Marygay allowed everyone ten minutes for goodbyes. Not many people took that long. After a little more than an hour, everybody was in the assembly area, watching a large flatscreen display of Marygay in the captain's chair. All 148 of us had maneuvered so as to be "lying" on the "floor" in front of the screen.

Marygay peered out of the screen, her thumb poised over a red button on the console. "Is everybody ready?" The crowd shouted yes and, with less than military precision, our journey began. (I wondered how many people were aware of the fact, or suspected, that the red button wasn't attached to anything. It was just an engineer's joke. The ship launched itself, and knew its time of departure to within a millionth of a second.)

The onset of acceleration was slow. I was floating about a foot off the floor, and I drifted down gently, and then gained weight over the course of ten or twelve seconds. There was a slight hum, which would be the background of all our lives for ten years: the tiny residue of the unimaginable sustained violence that was flinging us out of the galaxy.

I stood up and fell down. So did a lot of people, after days or weeks of zerogee. Sara took my arm and we helped each other up, laughing, forming a wobbly triangle with the floor, that closed up into two roughly parallel people. I cautiously lowered myself into a squat and stood up again, muscles and joints protesting.

About a hundred people were stepping around carefully, looking at their feet. The rest were sitting or lying down, some showing signs of anxiety or even panic.

They'd been told what to expect, that even breathing would seem to be an effort, at first. Those of us who'd been in and out of orbit the past months were used to it. But having it described to you and feeling it were two different things.

Marygay switched us over to a view of the planet. At first it just turned beneath us, a few wispy clouds over the mottled white snowscape. People were chatting and groaning in commiseration.

After a few minutes, things quieted down, as our motion became apparent. People sat and stared at the screen in silent meditation, perhaps a kind of hypnosis.

One curved horizon appeared, and then, on the opposite side of the screen, another. They inched toward one another until, after fifteen or twenty minutes, the planet was a huge ball, visibly shrinking.

Marygay had tottered down the stairs and was sitting next to me. "Goodbye, goodbye," she whispered, and I echoed her. But I think she was mostly saying goodbye to our son. I was saying goodbye to the planet and the time.

As it shrank away I felt an odd epiphany, born of science and mathematics. I knew that it would be a month—34.7 days—before we reached a tenth of the speed of light, and officially entered the realm of relativity. And it would be months later before the effect of it would be visible, looking out at the stars.

But we were actually there already. The huge force that made the ship's deck feel like a floor was already bending space and time. Our minds and bodies were not subtle enough to directly sense it yet. But that acceleration was slowly pulling us away from the mundane illusion we called reality.

Most of the matter and energy in the universe live in the land of relativity, because of extreme mass or speed. We would be joining them soon.

fourteen

We kept the image of Middle Finger centered on the screen for a couple of days, as it shrank to a dot, and then a bright star, and then was lost in the hot glow of Mizar. By the end of the first day, we didn't even have to filter Mizar's glare; it was just the brightest star in the sky.

People started going about their business. They knew that much of what they did was make-work; the ship, by necessity, could run itself. Even the agriculture, being integral to the life-support system, was closely monitored by the ship.

Sometimes it bothered me to know that the ship was intelligent and self-aware. It could greatly simplify its existence by turning off life support.

We, in turn, could override the ship. Marygay's captaincy, now largely symbolic, would suddenly become a real and huge burden. The *Time Warp* could be run without its brain, but it would be a daunting enterprise.

The fifteen children aboard did need parents and teachers, which gave some of us real work. I taught physical science and still had "father" in my job description, though most of my job there was keeping out of Sara's way.

Everybody who didn't have children had some other on-going project. A lot of them, of course, were engaged in creating and dissecting scenarios about what we were going to do forty thousand years from now. I couldn't get up much enthusiasm for that, myself. It seemed to me the only model worth planning about was the *tabula rasa* one, where we came back to find nothing left of humanity. Otherwise, we were Neanderthals speculating about starflight.

(The sheriff was in favor of a scenario where not much would change over forty thousand years, except increasing mastery over the physical universe. Why would Man want to change? I was more in favor of the one where Man, refusing to allow change, declines into gibbering savagery, in obedience to the Law of Increasing Entropy.)

There were several people writing histories of our voyage, whom I could visualize waiting hungrily for something bad to happen. No news is bad news for historians. Others were studying the social dynamics of our little group, which did seem worthwhile. Sociology with a uniquely reduced set of variables.

Others were writing compositions or novels, or otherwise engaged in the arts. Casi was already whittling away at his log, and on the second day out, Alysa Bertram announced she was holding auditions for a play that was in progress; the actors to collaborate on the script. Sara was one of the first to show up, and she was chosen. She wanted me to try out, but the idea of memorizing pages of dialogue always had sounded like mind-numbing torture to me.

Of course I did have my position on the council to keep me out of trouble. But we had a lot less to do, now that the voyage had begun.

With "gravity," the ship was a totally different place. In orbit, the floors were just nuisances, obstacles you had to swim around, and you thought of the ship in a sort of horizontal way, bow to stern, like a water ship. But now forward was up and aft was down. Less than an hour into the flight, Diana had to treat her first broken bone, when Ami—who had lived for months in zero-gee—instinctively tried to float down a staircase.

When that happened, I realized we didn't have anyone who was a safety inspector. So I gave myself the job, but wanted an assistant trained in civil engineering. One of the three people qualified was Cat. I guess I chose her so as not to appear to be avoiding her.

I didn't dislike Cat, though I'd never felt completely comfortable around her. Of course, she'd been born, if you can call it that, nine hundred years after me, into a world where heterosexuality was an affliction so rare most people never even encountered it. But the same was true of Charlie and Diana, our best friends.

Some were more hetero than others, though; Charlie'd had at least one fling with a guy. I wondered about Cat, who had left her husband behind. (Though at the time I'd been relieved; he was kind of worthless except for chess and go.)

Cat accepted the offer with enthusiasm. Most of her work was not really going to start for another ten years, when and if we had to roll up our sleeves and start building a new world.

We decided to work from top to bottom. There wasn't much

to be concerned about on the top floor, just cargo and control. Nobody would be going there regularly except for Marygay and her assistants, Jerrod Weston and Puül Ten. The five escape ships weren't locked, and I supposed people might sneak into them for privacy, so we checked them with that in mind.

There was not much inside them but acceleration couches and the suspended-animation pods. The couches looked safe enough, all padding, and I didn't think anyone would venture into the pods, unless they wanted to have sex in a dark coffin full of machinery. Cat said I lacked imagination.

The fourth floor was where most of the aquaculture was, so there was theoretical danger of drowning. All the tanks were shallow enough for adults to stand in with their heads above water, but most of the children were small enough for it to be a potential hazard. All the families with children lived on the first floor, but of course the kids would be roaming everywhere. The DON'T FEED THE FISH sign gave me an idea. I found Waldo Everest, who confirmed that the fish were fed a measured amount each day, and he agreed to go along with my plan: make the children responsible for actually scattering the feed. So the aquaculture pools would be their workplace, rather than a forbidden "attractive nuisance."

I'd never heard of that phrase until Cat used it. Describes some people well.

There were three shallow rice paddies which also were home to thousands of crayfish, not quite big enough for the menu yet. About half the floor area was given over to fast-growing grains, fish food. This floor smelled best to me, a whiff of the sea along with green growing things.

Not many safety hazards other than the fish ponds and some of the harvesting machinery. This was the stairwell where Ami fell and broke her arm, but it wasn't uniquely dangerous.

The elevator was right across from the stairs, 120 meters away, but you couldn't just walk across. The narrow path between the various hydroponic fields zigged and zagged. So we just walked around the sidewalk in front of the living quarters, which on this floor made up half a circumference of apartments, identical in size but with slightly different layouts.

The apartment where Marygay and I lived was right next to the elevator, a privilege of rank that was also a necessary convenience: the control room was directly overhead. I invited Cat in for tea. One apartment was as good as any other, to look over for safety hazards.

Compared to military quarters, the apartments were large. The ship was originally configured to hold 205 people, each one having one room four meters square. So our 150 were well spread out. Twenty-eight couples planned on having one or two children during the voyage, but even so, it wouldn't be especially crowded.

It did feel claustrophobic after our big house in Paxton, with the windows looking out on forest on one side and the broad lake behind. I put holo windows of the lake on the wall of our bedroom, but was thinking we ought to reset them. It looked real but felt false.

"Fire hazard," I said, putting the kettle on for tea. "Burn hazard, anyhow." The two burners were induction heaters, so you'd have to be really trying, to injure yourself.

"You have knives and things," Cat said. By choice, she didn't have a cooking area in her own place. Marygay and I had brought along enough kitchenware to cook and serve a meal for six, and a cabinet of precious spices and herbs. Up to a certain hour, by our tentative rules, you could go to the kitchen and get a meal's worth of raw materials, rather than show up for chow and have what everyone else was having.

"They say the bathroom's the most dangerous room in the house," she said. "Not much to worry about there." We had a toilet and small sink. Each floor had a shower room and a schedule, and there was a shower by the pool on the common floor.

The teapot chimed and I poured us each a cup, and sat next to her on the couch. I looked around the room critically. "Not much to worry about anywhere. You think about accidents at home—falls, cuts, burns, exposure to dangerous substances—and most of them involve things we don't have here."

She nodded. "Balanced by dangers we *don't* have at home. Like meteorites and life-support failures and the idea of standing on top of tonnes of antimatter."

"I'll make a note." We sipped in silence for an awkward minute. "Did you come along just to . . . just because of Marygay?"

She stared at me for a moment. "Partly. Partly because I knew Aldo wouldn't. It was an unembarrassing way to end the marriage." She set down her cup. "I also like the idea of running away, finding a new world. We weren't drafted, you know, in my time. I joined up to see new worlds. Middle Finger was getting pretty small." She made a wry smile. "Aldo really liked that. He fell in love with the farm."

"You're farming here, part time."

"Exercise. And I do know my root vegetables."

"I'm glad you came."

"You are." It was a question. "Aldo thought I was chasing after Marygay. Did he talk to you about that?"

"Not in so many words." But a lot of unsubtle innuendo.

"We do . . . I do love her." Cat was trying to keep a tremble out of her voice. "But I've been, we've been, sixteen years this way. Just neighbors, close neighbors. I'm content with that."

"I understand."

"I don't think you do. I don't think men *can*." She picked up her cup with both hands, as if to warm them. "Maybe that's not fair. I never met a het man until I was on Heaven, my mid-twenties. But the normal men and boys I grew up with always had to *do* each other. It wasn't serious if you weren't doing. Girls and women, it was different. You loved someone or you didn't. Whether you did each other was not a big deal."

"Yeah, I guess we were different. It's not het versus home. Women were more sexually aggressive in my time, too. But you were born, what, nine hundred years after I was?"

She nodded. "I think it was 2880, your style."

"I don't want to sound like a jealous husband," I said. "I know you and Marygay still love each other. It's obvious to any-one who cares."

"Then let's not worry about it. The lack of Aldo in my life is not going to drive me into her arms. Somebody's, maybe. But I'm as het as you are, remember?"

"Sure." I did wonder about that—how effective or perma-nent Man's technique actually was. I trusted Cat but did wonder. "More tea?"

"No, we ought to move along." She smiled. "People will start talking about us."

The third floor, the commons, did have safety problems that hadn't been obvious in zerogee. The carpeting in the caf-eteria was old and loose, inviting people with their hands full to trip. There was nothing to replace it with, of course. We pried up a corner and decided the metal deck would be preferable;

the dried adhesive was easy to peel off. I'd assemble a work crew in a few days.

We tested most of the apparatus in the fitness room, weight machines and stationary rowing, skiing, and pedaling ones. We looked at the rings and ropes and parallel bars and decided someone else could be the first to have an injury on them.

There were a lot of people already in the pool, including nine of the children. I knew the ship was watching that all day and night. The only people who lived on the commons floor were Lucio and Elena Monet, both expert swimmers with an apartment that overlooked the pool. One of them was always there, and could get to the pool in seconds if the ship sounded an alarm.

The first and second floors were drier versions of the fourth: 95 percent farm, ringed by apartments. The only water hazard was an oyster bed, so shallow you could only drown there in a prone position. (I had resisted activating the bed, which took six months to produce a crop, but was overridden by people who can actually look at an oyster without feeling ill.) Unlike the fourth floor, all of the apartments were one-story, so we didn't even have stairs to worry about.

The area under the first floor was the most dangerous part of the ship, but it was beyond the jurisdiction of the safety inspector and his trusty civil engineer. Seven tonnes of antiprotons seethed there in a glowing ball, held in place by a huge pressor field. If anything happened to the pressors, we would all have about one nanosecond to prepare ourselves for a new existence as highly energetic gamma rays.

Cat volunteered to take charge of the carpet demolition project, and I let her lead it, though I'd become accustomed to the role myself. For ten months, I'd been at the center of every-thing—arguing, coordinating, deciding—and now I was just another passenger. With a title and an amorphous job, but not in charge anymore. I had to get used to watching other people do it.

Marygay was theoretically on duty all the time, but in fact she only spent one eight-hour shift each day actually in the control room. Jerrod and Puül took the other two shifts.

Their physical presence in the control room was more a psychological, or social, need than an actual one. The ship always knew where all three were—and if there was a need for a quick decision, the ship would make it without consulting the humans. Human thought was too slow for emergencies, anyhow. Most of us passengers knew this, but it was comforting to have humans up there anyhow.

She liked studying the controls, a complex maze of read-outs, buttons, dials, and so forth, arrayed along a four-meter panel with two two-meter wings. She knew what everything was and did through her ALSC training, the way I knew how to fly a shuttle, but it was good to reinforce that crammed-in expertise with experience and observation in real time.

(One evening I asked her how many bells and whistles she thought there were on those eight meters of control board. She closed her eyes for about five minutes and then said, "One thousand two hundred thirty-eight.")

She chose to be on from 0400 to 1200, so we always met for lunch when she got off. We'd usually throw something together at our place, rather than go down to the "zoo," the cafeteria. Sometimes we'd have company. Back on MF we always had lunch with Charlie and Diana on Tuesdays, and saw no reason to change that ritual.

The second week out, I made potato and leek soup, for the first but not the last time—we'd be limited, for several months, to the vegetables Teresa and her crew had been able to grow in zerogee. So no tomatoes or lettuce for a few months.

Charlie showed up first, and we sat down to our ongoing chess game. One move apiece, and Marygay and Diana came in together.

Marygay looked at the board. "You ought to dust that every now and then."

I gave Diana a kiss. "How's the doctor business?"

"God, you don't want to know. I spent most of the morning exploring the rectum of one of your favorite people."

"Eloy?" I knew he had a problem.

She wagged a finger. "Confidentiality. I noticed a lot of vowels in his name, though."

Eloy Macabee was a strange abrasive man who called me almost every afternoon with some complaint or suggestion. He was the keeper of the chickens, though, so you had to give him some leeway. (Fish and chickens were the only animals we'd had aboard in zerogee. Fish can't tell the difference and chickens are too dumb to care.)

"Actually, you should know. Both of you," she said to Marygay as they both sat down at the table. "We have a small epidemic on our hands."

I turned up the heat on the soup and stirred it. "A virus?"

"I wish. A virus would be easy." Marygay poured coffee. "Thanks. It's depression. I've treated twenty-some people the last three days."

"That *is* an epidemic," Charlie said.

"Well, people do catch it from each other. And it can be deadly; suicide."

"But we expected it. Allowed for it," Marygay said.

"Not so soon, though, nor so many." She shrugged. "I'm not worried about it yet. Just puzzled."

I ladled the soup into bowls. "Do the victims have anything in common?"

"Unsurprisingly, it's mostly people who don't have real jobs, who aren't involved in the day-to-day running of things." She took a notebook out of her pocket and tapped a few numbers. "Just occurred to me . . . none of them are veterans, either."

"Not too surprising either," Charlie said. "At least we know what it's like, being cooped up together for years at a time."

"Yeah," I said, "but not *ten* years. You'll be seeing some of us before long."

"Good soup," Marygay said. "I don't know. I'm feeling more and more comfortable, now that I'm used to . . ."

"Bill," I said.

"Yes. Shipboard wasn't the worst part of the war. This is like 'old home week,' as we used to say. But without Taurans to worry about."

"One," Diana said. "But it's really no problem, not yet."

"Keeps to itself." I hadn't seen it five times.

"It must be lonely," Marygay said. "Separated from its group mind."

"Who knows what goes through their heads."

"Throats," Diana said.

I knew that. "Just an expression." I made the kissing sound for the ship. "Continue Mozart." Soft strains of a lute being chased by woodwinds.

"He was German?" Diana said.

I nodded. "Maybe Prussian."

"He was still being played in our time. It sounds strange to my ear, though."

I called the ship again. "How much of your music comes from before the twentieth century?"

"In playing time, about seven percent. In titles, about five percent."

"Good grief. Only one out of twenty I can listen to."

"You ought to sample the others," Charlie said. "Classicism and romanticism return in cycles."

I nodded, but kept my opinion to myself. I had sampled a few centuries. "Maybe we should switch jobs around. Give the depressed people something significant to do."

"Could help. We wouldn't want to be too obvious about it."

"Sure," Marygay said. "Put dysfunctional people in *all* the important positions."

"Or put them in suspended animation," Charlie said. "Table the problem for forty thousand years."

"Don't think I haven't considered asking for that."

"We couldn't just tell everybody there's a problem?" I said. "They're intelligent adults."

"In fact, two of the patients are children. But no; I think that would cause even more depression and anxiety.

"The problem is that depression, and anxiety for that matter, are both behavioral problems and biochemical ones. But you don't want to treat a short-term problem by altering a person's brain chemistry. We'd wind up with a ship full of addicts. Including the four of us."

"The mad leading the mad," Charlie said.

"Ship of fools," Marygay said.

I kissed for the ship and asked, "If we all went insane, would you be able to carry out the mission?"

"Some of you are already insane, though perhaps my standards are too high. Yes, if the captain so ordered, I could lock the controls and conduct the mission without human mediation."

"And if the captain were insane?" Marygay asked. "And the two co-captains?"

"You know the answer to that, Captain."

"I do," she said quietly, and took a sip of wine. "And you know what? I find it depressing."

sixteen

The next day, we had something more depressing to worry
about than depression.

I was in my office on the common floor, doing the flunky
job of tallying people's requests for various movies for afternoon
and evening showings. Most of them I'd never heard of. Two
people asked for *A Night to Remember* and *Titanic,* which would
do wonders for morale. Space icebergs. Hadn't worried about
them in days.

The Tauran appeared at my door. I croaked a greeting at
it, and glanced at my watch. Five minutes later and I would have
escaped to lunch.

"I did not know whether to bring this problem to you or
the captain or the sheriff." The sheriff? "You were closest."

"What problem?"

It made an agitated little dance. "A human has tried to kill me."

"Good God!" I stood up. "Who is it?"

"He is the one called Charlton."

Cal, of course. "Okay. I'll get the sheriff and we'll go find him."

"He is in my quarters, dead."

"You killed him?"

"Of course. Wouldn't you?"

I called Marygay and the sheriff and told them to come down immediately. "Were there any witnesses?"

"No. He was alone. He said he wanted to talk to me."

"Well, the ship will have seen it."

It bobbed its head. "To my knowledge, the ship does not monitor my quarters."

I kissed for the ship and asked it. "That's correct. The Tauran's quarters were improvised out of storage. I was not designed to monitor storage."

"Did you see Cal Charlton headed in that direction recently?"

"Charlton got on the lift at 11:32 and it went down to the storage level."

"Was he armed?"

"I could not tell."

"He tried to kill me with an axe," the Tauran said. "I heard glass break, and he came running in. He got the axe from the fire station outside my quarters."

"Ship, can you confirm that?"

"No. If he had pulled the fire alarm, I would have known that." Well, that was an interesting fact.

"So you took the axe away from him?"

"It was simple. I heard the glass break, and correctly inter-preted that. I stepped behind the door. He never saw me."

"So you killed him with the axe."

"Not actually. I believe I broke his neck." It demonstrated with a convincing karate-like stroke.

"Well, that's . . . it could be worse."

"Then, to be sure, I took the axe and severed his head." It made a gesture like a shrug. "That's where the brain is."

You don't want to be disrespectful of the dead, but it was a good thing the Tauran hadn't killed someone anybody liked. Cal was kind of a loose cannon when he was younger, and although he seemed to have calmed down in recent years, he did have outbursts. Married three times, never for very long. In retrospect, it's clear we shouldn't have brought him along; if he hadn't been in on it from the beginning, he probably wouldn't have been chosen, in spite of his many useful talents.

He was one of Diana's depression patients, it turned out, but when we looked over his belongings we found that he had taken one pill and then quit. Two days later, he tried to kill Antres 906.

If everyone aboard had liked Cal, we would have had a lynch mob. As it was, the council agreed with the sheriff that it was an unambiguous case of self-defense, and there was no pub-lic disagreement with that. So we were spared the knotty prob-lem of a trial between species. No Tauran had ever committed a crime on MF. Antres 906 claimed that the Taurans had no equivalent to the human legal system, and it appeared to me that it didn't really grasp what a trial *was*. If there are no indi-

viduals in your race, what constitutes crime and punishment—
or morality or ethics, for that matter?

Anyhow, Antres 906 was in a kind of existential solitary con-
finement already, by choice. Whatever "choice" means to a
Tauran; I suppose they normally have their equivalent of the
Whole Tree, and just follow its orders without question.

In solitary, but not alone. One of the council was always
with it for several days after the killing, protecting it, armed with
the tranquilizer rifle. It was a lot more time than I'd ever spent
with a Tauran, and Antres 906 didn't mind talking.

One time, I brought along the five-page document from
Earth, sentencing us to stay out of space. I asked it about that
mysterious last line: "Inside the foreign, the unknown; inside
that, the unknowable."

"I don't understand this," I said. "Is it supposed to be a
general statement about reality?"

It rubbed its neck in an almost human gesture, which I
knew meant *I'm thinking*. "No. Not at all." It lightly ran its long
finger over the Braille twice more.

"Our languages are very different, and the written language
is subtle. The translation is incomplete, because . . ." It rubbed
the line again.

"I don't understand human jokes, but I think this is something like a joke. When you say something and mean something
different."

"What words would you use?"

"Words? The words are accurate. They are familiar, a saying
in what you would call our religion.

"But when we use them, they are not inflected this way,
which is what makes me think of your jokes. The word 'unknowable' here, it means, or rhymes with, 'un-namable,' or 'nameless.' Which is sort of like fate, or God, in human terms."

"It's supposed to be funny?"

"Not at all, no, not in this inflection." It handed the paper back to me. "Normally, it is meant to be an expression about the complexity of the universe."

"That's reasonable enough."

"But this inflection is not a generalization. It's directed at you, I suppose the one hundred forty-eight of you. Or maybe even all humans. And it is . . . an admonition? A warning."

I read the English again. "Warning that we're headed for the unknowable?"

"Either that or the other way around: the unknowable is headed for you. The nameless."

I thought about that. "It could just be talking about relativity, then. It gets pretty mysterious."

It scraped out a syllable of negation. "Not for us."

seventeen

I t was little things at first. No pattern.

A whole bed of oysters stopped growing. The other beds were okay. It only interested me academically, since I had an oyster once and decided once would do it for me. But I helped Xuan and Shaunta run environmental tests, having been a fish farmer in another life, myself, and there wasn't one molecule of difference that we could detect between the affected bed and the others. There didn't seem to be anything wrong with the oysters, except that they refused to grow beyond thumbnail size.

We finally decided to sacrifice the bed and harvest them immature, making about ten liters of soup, which I declined to savor. Then we drained and sterilized the pool and reseeded it.

All the movies and cubes that began with the letter *C* were missing. No *Casablanca* or *Citizen Kane*. But an article would preserve them, so we still had *The Cat Women from Mars* and *A Cunt for All Seasons,* so some ancient culture was preserved.

Little things.

The temperature regulator on the children's pool refused to work. It would run hot one day and not at all the next. Lucio and Elena took it apart and put it back together, and so did Matthew Anderson, who had an affinity with such things. But it never did work, and Elena took it out of the system altogether after she tested the water one morning and it was scalding. The kids didn't seem to mind the cold water, but it made them a little more noisy.

Something happened to the floor of the handball court. It got tacky; it was like trying to move around on half-dried glue. We stripped it and revarnished it, but of course it was the same varnish, and soon after it dried, it became tacky again.

That wouldn't have seemed important; just an unfortunate choice of materials, but it was the same varnish we used on *all* of the ship's fiber surfaces, and it only had gotten tacky in that one location. Handball players do sweat. As if weight lifters did not.

Then a small thing happened that had no reasonable explanation at all. It could only have been an elaborate but pointless practical joke: the air was sucked out of a food storage locker.

Rudkowski sent a report to me, annoyed, and I went down to look at the thing. It was a grain storage locker, free-standing, with no possible connection to vacuum.

There's no lock on the door, but when Rudkowski, a strong, fat man, had gone to open it, it wouldn't budge. Another cook helped him pull on it, and it jerked open suddenly, with a sucking inrush of air. Same thing happened the next day, and so he sent up the report.

We emptied out the locker and went over it minutely, and even had Antres 906 come up and use his differently acute senses. The only way for the thing to lose air would be for somebody to pump it out, but none of us could find any opening.

"Fearsome," was the Tauran's only reaction. We were still annoyed, rather than scared. But then we had the locker watched all afternoon and night. No one came near it, but by the next morning it was full of vacuum again.

Against the obscure possibility of conspiracy, I stood watch over it all night myself, drinking what passed for coffee. The air disappeared again.

Word got out about this strangeness, and reactions were diverse. Some stolid people—or people in ignorant denial—didn't think it was a big deal. The locker was small, and the daily air loss from it was not even 1 percent of what we lost through normal accepted leakage. If we left it closed, we wouldn't even lose that.

Other people were terrified, and I had some sympathy with them. Since we didn't know what mechanism was sucking air out of the small space, how could we know that the same mechanism might not empty out whole rooms, whole floors—the entire ship!

Teresa Larson and her co-religionists were actually smug: here was something going on that the scientists and engineers couldn't explain. Something mystical, that was happening for a purpose, and God would reveal Her purpose in due course. I asked her whether she would like to spend the night in the grain locker, to test God's sympathy with her belief. She patiently explained the fallacy behind my logic. If you "tested" God, that was the direct opposite of belief, and of course She would punish you.

I kept my silence about that elaboration of foolishness. I like Teresa, and she is probably the best farmer aboard, but her grasp of reality beyond the tilled field or hydroponic tank is seriously impaired.

Most people were in the same middle ground that I inhabited. Something serious was going on that we didn't yet understand. For now, the practical course was to seal the locker and store the grain elsewhere, while people mulled it over.

The most disturbing reaction was from Antres 906. It asked for permission to do a complete systems check on the escape vessels, with the help of a few human engineers. It said we would need them soon.

Antres 906 approached me first. If it had been a human, I would have said no; we're close enough to panic, and don't need to fuel it. But Tauran logic and emotion are odd, so I took him up to Marygay for a captain's decision.

Marygay was reluctant to grant special permission, since of course we did have a regular inspection schedule, and it *could* look like panic. But there was no actual harm in it, so long as it was done quietly, as if it were routine. And she did have sympathy for Antres 906 in its isolation. A human locked in a ship with a hundred Taurans would be forgiven for odd behavior.

But when she asked it to elaborate on why it thought the inspection was necessary, the response was creepy.

"Not long ago, William asked me about that piece of paper? The one from Earth? 'Inside the foreign, the unknown; inside that, the unknowable.' "

It did the little Tauran dance of agitation. "We *are* inside the foreign. Your airless locker represents the unknown."

"Wait," I said. "Are you saying that that homily is a kind of prophecy?"

"No, never." The dance again. "Prophecy is foolish. What it is, is a statement of condition."

Marygay stared at him. "You're saying we should be ready for the unknowable."

It rubbed its neck and rattled assent and danced, and danced.

book four

THE BOOK OF
THE DEAD

eighteen

I t took two months for the unknowable to catch up with us.

Marygay and I were asleep. A chime woke us up.

"Sorry, but I have to disturb you."

Marygay sat up and touched the light. "Me?" she said, rubbing her eyes. "What's wrong?"

"Both of you. We're losing fuel."

"Losing *fuel?*"

"It began less than a minute ago. The antimatter is steadily decreasing in mass. As I speak, we have lost about one half of one percent."

"Good God," I said. "What, is it leaking?" And if so, how come we still exist?

"It is not physically leaking. It is in some way disappearing, though." It made a rare humming sound, that meant it was thinking. It thought so fast it could solve most problems between phonemes.

"I can say with certainty that it is not leaking. If it were, the antiprotons would be receding from us at one gee. I sprayed water back along our path, and there was no reaction."

I didn't know whether that was good or bad. "Have you sent a message to Middle Finger?"

"Yes. But if it continues at this rate, the antimatter will be gone long before they receive it."

Of course; we were more than four light-days away. "Charge up every fuel cell to the maximum."

"I did that as we were speaking."

"How long . . ." Marygay said, "how long can we last on auxiliary power?"

"About five days, at the normal rate of consumption. Several weeks, if we close off most life support and confine everybody to one floor."

"We're still losing it?"

"Yes. The rate of loss appears to be increasing. If this continues, we will be out of fuel in twenty-eight minutes."

"Should we sound the general alarm?" I asked Marygay.

"Not yet. We have enough to worry about."

"Ship, do you have any idea where the fuel could be going; whether we could get it back?"

"No. Nothing consistent with physics as I know it. There is an analogy in the Rhomer model for transient-barrier virtual particle substitution, but it has never been demonstrated." I'd have to look that up sometime.

"Wait!" Marygay said. "The escape ships. Is their antimatter evaporating, too?"

"Not yet. But it is not transferable."

"I'm not thinking about transferring it," she said to me. "I'm thinking about getting the hell out of here before something worse happens."

"Very sensible," the ship said.

We put on robes and hurried down to the first floor. From the viewing port we could see the antimatter sphere as it shrank. It otherwise didn't look any different, a ball of blue sparkles, but it did grow smaller and smaller. Finally, it blinked out.

Acceleration stopped and the automatic zerogee cables unreeled, with a soft regular chiming, loud enough to wake most of the people. We could hear a few louder bells from some residences.

We'd done zerogee drill five times, twice unannounced, so it was not a big deal, yet. People floated out of their homes in various states of undress and started monkey-climbing to the common floor's assembly area.

Eloi Casi, the sculptor, was fully dressed, with a work apron covered with wood shavings. "Damned silly time to pull a drill, Mandella. I'm trying to work."

"Wish it was a drill, Eloi." We drifted past him.

"What?"

"No power. No antimatter. No choices."

Those six words were about all we could tell the company assembled, with the ship adding numbers and times.

"We might as well zip up in the escape ships and get the hell out of here," Marygay said. "Every second we delay, it's another twenty-four thousand kilometers we have to make up."

"We're going eight percent of the speed of light," I said. "The escape ships have a slow steady thrust of 7.6 centimeters per second, squared. It will take us ten years to slow down to zero, and another fourteen to get back to MF."

"Why do we have to rush it?" Alysa Bertram said. "That antimatter might come back as mysteriously as it disappeared."

"Yeah, suppose it does?" Stephen Funk said, coming to my elbow. "Do you want to rely on it then? What if it went fine for another couple of months and then disappeared for good? You want to risk ten thousand years in suspended animation?"

Antres 906 had entered, and was floating just inside the door. I looked its way and it bobbed its head: *Who knows?*

"I agree with Steve," I said. "Show of hands? How many want to zip up and leave?"

Slightly more than half the hands went up. "Wait a minute here," Teresa Larson said. "I haven't had my god-damned coffee yet, and you want me to decide whether to give all this up and go flinging into space?"

Nobody had put more work into revitalizing the ship. "I'm sorry, Teresa. But I watched the stuff disappear, and I don't see any alternative."

"Maybe it's our faith being tested, William. Though you wouldn't know anything about that."

"No, I wouldn't. But I don't think the antimatter's going to come back just because we really, sincerely want it to."

"Those escape ships are death traps," Eloy Macabee whined. "How many people die in SA, one out of three? Four?"

"Suspended animation has a survival rate of over eighty percent," I said. "The survival rate here aboard ship is going to be zero."

Diana had come up to float beside me. "The less time we spend in SA, the more likely we are to survive. Teresa, you have your cup of coffee. But then come down and get in line. I'm going to prep people as quickly as possible."

"We aren't accelerating anymore," Ami Larson said. "We can afford to wait and think things over."

"Okay—you hang around and think," Diana said heatedly. "I want out of here before something else happens. Like the air disappearing, next—you want to think *that* one over, Ami? You want to tell me it couldn't happen?"

"If people do want to stay till the last minute," I said, "you can't expect Diana to wait along with you."

"They can prep themselves, without a doctor or nurse," she said. "But if anything goes wrong, they just die."

"In their sleep," Teresa said.

"I don't know. Maybe you wake up long enough to strangle. Nobody's ever come back to report."

Marygay stepped into the moment of hostile silence. She had a clipboard. "I want names of people willing to leave on the first and second ships. That's sixty people. You can take at most three kilograms of personal items. First group, show up at ten o'clock."

To Diana: "How long does it take to prepare?"

"The purging part is like lightning. You want to be sitting on a toilet when you take the medicine." Some people laughed nervously. "Seriously. Then it takes maybe five minutes to hook up the orthotics. Those of us who did high-gee combat used to do it in under a minute. But we're out of practice."

"And a little older now. So figure the second group at noon?"

"That's reasonable. Nobody eat anything between now and then, and don't drink anything but water. Don't take any medicine unless you clear it with me."

The clipboard started around. "Once I get these sixty names," Marygay said, "the ones who've signed up can go. Then we'll start filling ships Three and Four. How many people are dead-set against going?" Twenty people raised hands, some tentatively. I think Paul Greyton and Elena Monet did it out of fear of going against their spouses. Or maybe reluctance to leave them. "Come over here with me and William, to the coffee station."

No more coffee from this gravity-fed machine, ever again. That was a plus.

Marygay kissed for the ship. "What chance do these people have for survival?"

"I can't calculate that, Captain. I don't know where the antimatter went, so I don't know what the probability is that it might reappear."

"How long will they live if it stays missing?"

"If the twenty people stayed in this one room, and kept it insulated, they could live for many years. My water will begin to freeze in a few weeks, though, and one person will have to go out to the pool and mine it.

"But the pool has enough water for ten years, if you only drink it, and don't wash.

"Food is the complicating factor. Before the first year is over, you'll have to resort to cannibalism. Of course, with each person harvested, there is one less person to feed, and the average body should yield about three hundred meals. So the final survivor will have lived one thousand sixty-four days after the first one is killed, assuming he or she stays warm."

Marygay was silent for a moment, smiling. "Think it over." She kicked off from the table and floated toward the door. I followed, less gracefully.

There was a private command line outside the cafeteria door. I picked up the handset, and said, "Ship, do you have a sense of humor?"

"Only in that I can distinguish between incongruous situations and sensible ones. That was incongruous."

"What are you going to do when everyone is gone?"

"I have no choice but to wait."

"For what?"

"For the return of the antimatter."

"You actually think it will come back?"

"I didn't 'actually' think it would disappear. I have no idea where it is. Whatever agency caused it to relocate may be constrained by some physical conservation law."

"So you wouldn't be surprised if it reappeared."

"I'm never surprised."

"And if it *does* come back?"

"I'll return to Middle Finger, to my parking orbit. With some new data for you physicists."

Nobody had called me a physicist in a long time. I'm a science teacher and fish harvester and vacuum welder. "I'll miss you, Ship."

"I understand," it said, and made a noise like a throat clearing. "In your game with Charles, you should move the queen's rook to QR6. Then sacrifice your remaining knight to the pawn, and move the black bishop up to checkmate."

"Thanks. I'll try to remember that."

"I'll miss everybody," it said without prompting. "I do have plenty of information to move around and recombine; enough to keep busy for a long time. But it's not the same as the constant chaotic input from you."

"Goodbye, Ship."

"Goodbye, William."

There was a line floating for the lift. I clambered down the steps hand-over-hand, feeling athletic.

I realized I had shifted into an emotional mode reminiscent of combat. Something over which I had no control had suddenly put me into a situation where I had a 20 percent chance of dying. Instead of apprehension, I felt a kind of resignation, and even impatience: let's get this over with, one way or the other.

Did I have three kilograms of stuff I wanted to take back to MF? The old book of paintings from the Louvre—I'd picked that up from a pile of Earth artifacts when I left Stargate for Middle Finger, a fairly new thousand-year-old antique. That wasn't even a kilogram. I'd brought along my comfortable boots in case there were no cobblers forty thousand years in the future. But with only twenty-four years passing, Herschel Wyatt would probably still be at his last.

I wondered who would be fishing my trotlines. Not Bill. He would probably be in Centrus by now, totally integrated into Man. Hell, he might even have gone to Earth.

We might never see him again. That felt different now. I shook my head and four tiny globules of tears floated away from my lashes.

Marygay and I, along with the rest of the council and Diana and Charlie, waited till the last. The last shuttle was almost half empty: thirteen people had elected to stay behind.

Teresa Larson was their spokeswoman, still staying though her wife Ami was asleep aboard the second ship. Their daughter Stel was staying with Teresa; their other daughter was on MF.

"For me, there's no decision," she said. "God sent us on this pilgrimage, to come back and start anew. She interrupted our progress in order to test our faith."

"You aren't going to start anew," Diana said. "You have ten

thousand sperm and ova frozen, but not one of you knows how to thaw them out and combine them."

"We'll make babies the old way," she said bravely. "Besides, we have plenty of time to study. We'll learn your arts."

"No, you won't. You'll starve or freeze right here. God didn't take that antimatter away, and it's not coming back."

Teresa smiled. "You're only saying that on faith. You don't know any more about it than I do. And my faith is as good as yours."

I wanted to shake some sense into her. Actually, I wanted to hunt them all down with the tranquilizer darts and load them aboard the ship unconscious. Almost everybody disagreed with me, though, and Diana wasn't sure that they could be hooked up properly without being conscious and cooperating.

"I'll pray for you all," Teresa said. "I hope you all survive and find a good life back home."

"Thank you." Marygay looked at her watch. "Now go back to your people and tell them that at 0900 the ship will seal this door and evacuate the chamber. We can take anybody, everybody until 0800. After that, you just stay here and . . . take your chances."

"I want to go with you," Diana said. "One last chance to talk some sense into them."

"No," Teresa said. "We've heard you, and the ship has repeated your argument twice." To Marygay: "I'll tell them what you said. We appreciate your concern." She turned and floated away.

There was only one zerogee toilet. Stephen Funk came out of it looking pale. "Your turn, William."

The stuff tasted like honey with a dash of turpentine. The effect was an internal scalding waterfall.

In school, in anthropology, we read about an African tribe that lived all year on bread and milk and cheese. Once a year, they butchered a cow to gorge themselves on fat, because they thought diarrhea was a gift from the gods, a holy cleansing. They would have loved *this* stuff. Even I felt holier. In fact, I felt like one big empty hole.

I cleaned up and floated out. "Have fun, Charlie. It's a moving experience."

I floated and clambered over to the last escape ship, with its thirty coffins lined up in dim red light. Was this the last thing I would ever see? I could think of more pleasant scenes.

Diana helped me hook up the orthotics, with a lubricant that contained a muscle relaxant. It was easier than the last time, coming back from the last battle. I suppose they had learned something over the centuries.

A slap on my left leg numbed it from the groin down. I knew this was the last one, the shunt that would replace my blood with a slippery polymer.

"Wait," Marygay said, and she leaned over the coffin and held my face in both hands, and kissed me. "See you tomorrow, darling."

I couldn't think of anything to say, and just nodded, already getting dreamy.

nineteen

I didn't know that five of Teresa's gang had a change of heart, and joined my pod at the last minute. I was already in the strange space I would occupy for the next twenty-four years.

All five ships were ejected from the *Time Warp* simultaneously, so they would have a chance of arriving back home within a few days or weeks of one another. A difference in thrust down in the seventh or eighth decimal place could make a big difference in arrival time, multiplied over twenty-four years.

We basically pointed our noses in the direction of Middle Finger and patiently ate away velocity for ten years. At some point, for one instant, we were absolutely still, with respect to the home planet. Then for seven years we accelerated toward it, and flipped, and for another seven years slowed back down.

Of course I felt none of this. Time passed quickly—far too fast to be almost half as long as my life—but I could tell it was passing. I was neither quite awake nor asleep, it seemed to me afterwards, but floating in a kind of sea of remembrance and fantasy.

For many years, or year-long days, I was obsessed with the notion that all of my life since the Aleph-null campaign, or Yod-4 or Tet-2 or Sade-138, was being lived in the instant between a fatal wounding and death: all those billions of neurons basking in their last microsecond of existence, running through a finite, but very large, combination of possibilities. I would not live forever, but I wouldn't really die as long as the neurons kept firing and seeking.

Coming awake was like dying—all that had been real for so long slowly fading into blindness and deafness and the chill numbing that had been my body's actual state for decades.

I vomited dry air, over and over.

When my stomach and lungs were tired of that, a tube inside my mouth misted something sweet and cool. I tried to open my eyes, but damp pads held them gently shut.

Two delicious stings as the orthotics withdrew, and the first motion of my limbs, if you count a twig as a limb, was a fast erection in reaction to warm blood. I couldn't move my arms or legs for some time. Fingers and toes made satisfying crackly sounds, coming to life.

Diana lifted the pads from my eyes and pried the lids apart with dry fingers. "Hello? Anybody home?"

I swallowed thin syrup, and coughed weakly. "Is Marygay all right?" I croaked.

"Resting. I just woke her a few minutes ago. You're second."

"Where are we? Are we here?"

"Yes, we're here. When you're able to sit up, you'll see good old MF down there, looking cold as a bitch." I strained, but was only able to rock a few inches. "Don't knock yourself out. Just rest for a while. When you get hungry, you can have some ancient soup."

"How many ships?"

"I don't know how to hail them. When Marygay gets up, she or you can give them a call. I can see one."

"How many people? Did we lose any to SA?"

"One. Leona; I've kept her frozen. There might be disabilities among the others, but they're waking up."

I slept for a couple of hours and then woke to the low murmur of Marygay's voice on the horn. I sat up in my coffin and Diana brought me some broth. It tasted like carrots and salt.

She unlatched the side. My clothes were where I had left them, twenty-four years older but still in style. I had to stop halfway through dressing to swallow hard a few times, coping with zerogee nausea. It wasn't too bad. I remembered the first time, back in graduate school, when I was useless for a couple of days. Now I just swallowed until the soup remembered to stay down, and finished dressing and floated up to join Marygay.

She was half-sitting, in a zerogee crouch, in the pilot's station. I strapped myself in next to her.

"Darling."

She looked bad, both haggard and bloated, and from her expression I knew I looked the same. She leaned over and kissed me, carrot-flavored.

"It's not good," she said. "This ship lost track of Number Four years ago. Number Two is more than a week behind, for some reason."

"It thinks Number Four's dead?"

"Doesn't have an opinion." She chewed her lower lip. "Seems likely. Eloi and the Snells. I haven't checked the roster, who else is on board."

"Cat's on Two," I said unnecessarily.

"It's probably okay." She stabbed at a button. "We have another little problem. Can't get Centrus."

"The spaceport?"

"The spaceport, no. Nothing else, either."

"Could it be the radio?"

"I get the other two ships. But they're close. Maybe it's a power thing."

"Maybe." I didn't think so. If the radio worked at all, it would pull in pretty weak signals. "Tried a visual search?"

She shook her head, one jerk. "The optical gear's on Number Four. We've got sperm and ova and shovels." Mass was critical, of course, and the planet-building stuff was distributed among the five ships with only enough duplication so that the loss of one ship wouldn't doom all the others.

"I got some sort of carrier wave when I first turned it on. The ship thinks it's one of the Centrus shuttles, in a medium-low orbit. Should be back in an hour or so." We were in geosynch, high up.

I looked at the cold white ball of MF, and remembered warm California. If we had gone to Earth twenty-some years ago, forty-some now, it would be warm and safe. No children to worry over or grieve.

Somebody was vomiting loudly. I unsnapped the vacuum cleaner from the back of the copilot's chair and kicked aft to deal with it.

It's not too bad if you work fast. It was Chance Delany, who looked more sheepish than sick.

"Sorry," he said. "It didn't want to get past my throat."

"Drink water for a while," I said, buzzing up the little globules. As if I were an expert.

I filled him in on the situation. "Good God. You don't think the Mother Earth people got in power?"

That was Teresa's crowd. "No. Even if they did, Man wouldn't let them shut everything down."

In another hour, the rest of the council was up—Sage, Steve, and Anita. Marygay and I were starting to look more normal, as our faces filled in and tightened up.

"Okay," Marygay said, touching a viewscreen. "I've got it again. It's a shuttle, all right."

"Well, I'm the pilot. Let's go get it and see what's happening downstairs." We couldn't simply land the escape vessels as if they were overgrown shuttles—or, rather, we *could*, but the exhaust would kill any humans or animals not under cover for a radius of several kilometers.

"Let's wait until everyone's been up for a couple of hours. We ought to use the acceleration couches, in case."

"Can you see it?" Anita asked.

"Not from here. But it is there; the signal's pretty strong."

"Only one?" Steve said.

"I think so. If there's another one in orbit, it's not broadcasting." She came back hand-over-hand to where we were floating. "We should maneuver all three ships into echelon, for safety, and approach it in formation."

"Good," I said. You had to be careful where you pointed the gamma-ray exhaust, even in space. If all three were parallel, we were safe.

"No one aboard the shuttle?" Chance asked.

"I don't get any voice response. They would've seen us arriving." We'd be brighter than Alcor, coming in. "There might be something wrong with our radio. But I don't think so. I do pick up the carrier wave, and that's the frequency they'd use."

She sighed, and shook her head. "We better hope it's the radio," she said softly. "I don't pick up anything at all, in any broadcast frequency. It's as if . . ."

"But it's only been twenty-four years," Steve said.

Anita finished the thought. "Not long enough for everyone to die out."

"I don't suppose it takes too long," Chance said. "Not if you work at it."

"You know," I said, "it's just possible everybody left."

"In what?" Steve gestured at the square of sky. "We took the only ship."

"Man said there were thousands parked back by Earth. It would be a huge undertaking, but if they had to, they could evacuate Middle Finger in less than a year."

"Some ecological catastrophe," Marygay said. "All those mutations, the crazy weather."

"Or another war," Chance said. "Not with the Taurans. There are probably worse ones out there."

"We'll know soon enough," I said. "They probably left a note. Or a lot of bones."

twenty

It took ten hours to maneuver the three ships to within reach of the shuttle, skimming three hundred kilometers over the planet's surface. I got into the roomy one-size-fits-everybody space suit and, after a clumsy hug from Marygay, managed to jet myself from airlock to airlock with only one overshoot.

The readout over my eye said the shuttle's air was good, temperature cold but liveable, so I climbed out of the big suit and called the other two over. I had decided to take Charlie down, and, in case there was something Man could understand better than us, the sheriff. I would have taken Antres 906 if it could have been squeezed into the suit. The Taurans may have left a Braille note saying, "Die, human scum," or something.

I asked the shuttle what was going on, but got no answer. Not surprising; it didn't need a lot of brainpower to maintain a low parking orbit. But under normal circumstances, it would automatically have tapped into a brain planetside, to answer my questions.

I'd sort of expected grisly skeletons sitting in the acceleration couches. But there was no sign of human habitation, except for some coveralls floating around loose. I assumed the shuttle had been sent into orbit under autopilot.

After Charlie and the sheriff made their way over, and stashed the three suits and got everybody strapped in, I punched in the one-digit command for "Return to Centrus." (So much for weeks in the ALSC machine.) The shuttle waited eleven minutes, and then began to angle down into the atmosphere.

We approached the small spaceport from the east, over the exurbs of Vendler and Greenmount. It was early thaw, snow still on the ground. The sun was coming up, but there was no smoke rising from chimneys. No floaters or people in evidence.

There were only two allowable landing paths, dead east and dead west, both fenced off from horizon to horizon. That wasn't out of fear of crashing, although that might have occurred to somebody. Its primary function was to protect people from the shuttle's gamma-ray exhaust, taking off.

The horizontal landing was smooth. Not a peep from the control tower. No floater came out to greet us, surprise. I popped the airlock and a light staircase spidered down.

Gravity was both reassuring and tiring. Our flight suits were not quite thick enough for the damp cold, and we were all shivering—even the genetically perfect sheriff—by the time we'd covered the kilometer back to the main building.

It was almost as cold inside, but at least there was no wind.

The offices were deserted and dusty. As far as we could tell, there was no power in the building. There was little disorder, just a few paper spills and drawers left open. No sign of panic or violence—no unsightly clutter of bodies or bones.

No notes written in the dust either: BEWARE, THE END IS NIGH. It was as if everybody had stepped out for lunch and kept going.

But they had left their clothes behind.

All along the corridors and behind most of the desks were tired bundles of clothing, as if each person had stopped where they were, undressed, and left. Flattened by years of gravity, stiff and dusty, most of the clothing was still identifiable. Business clothes and work coveralls, and a few uniforms. All of the inner and outer clothing piled on top of shoes.

"This is . . ." For once, Charlie was at a loss for words.

"Scary," I said. "I wonder if it's just here, or everywhere."

"I think everywhere," the sheriff said, and squatted down. He came up with a gaudy diamond ring, an obvious Earth antique. "No scavengers came through here."

Mystery or no, we were all famished, and searched out the cafeteria.

We didn't bother with the refrigerator and freezer, but found a pantry with some boxes of fruit, meat, and fish. After a quick meal, we split up to search the place for some clue as to how long it had been deserted; what had happened.

The sheriff found a yellowed newspaper, dated 14 Galileo 128. "As we might have guessed," he said. "The same day we started back, allowing for relativity."

"So they disappeared the same time that our antimatter did." My watch beeped, reminding me that it was almost time for Marygay to pass overhead. The three of us were just able to push open an emergency door.

The sky was slightly hazy, or we might have been able to see the escape ships as three close white spots drifting across the sky.

We were only able to talk for a few minutes, but there wasn't that much to say. "Two unexplainable things happening at the same time most likely had the same cause."

She said they'd continue a visual inspection from orbit. They didn't have anything sophisticated, but Number Three had powerful binoculars. They could see our shuttle and the line it had made in the snow, landing, and the other shuttle, conspicuous under a snow-shedding tarpaulin.

The escape ships would have to land on their tails, so there had better be no one living within a few kilometers of where they came down—else there *would* be no one living. Our shuttle's gamma-ray blast wasn't 1 percent of the larger ships'.

It looked like that wouldn't be a problem.

If there were people living in town, we'd have to go out into the country and find an alternative landing spot big enough and flat enough. I could think of a couple of farms I wouldn't mind seeing put to that use, just for old times' sake.

We found cold-weather gear in a locker room in the basement, bright orange coveralls that were lightweight and oily to the touch. I knew that it wasn't oil, just some odd polymer that trapped a millimeter of vacuum between the suit's layers, but they still felt greasy.

Hoping against hope, we went into the service garage, but the vehicles' fuel cells were all dead. The sheriff remembered about an emergency vehicle, though, that we found parked outside. Designed to work in situations where power wasn't available, it had a small plutonium reactor.

It was an ungainly garish thing, a bright yellow box set up for firefighting, remote rescue, and immediate medical aid. It was wide enough inside for six beds, with room for nurses or surgeons to move around them.

Getting into it was a problem, the doors locked shut with

ice. We got a couple of heavy screwdrivers from the garage and chipped our way inside.

The lights came on when the door opened, a good sign. We turned the defroster on high and looked around—a handy mobile base of operations, now and when the rest of the crowd came down, as long as the plutonium held out.

A "remaining hours of operation" readout said 11,245. I wondered how to interpret that, since it probably used more power charging up a mountainside than sitting here with its lights on.

When the windshield was clear, the sheriff sat down in the driver's seat. Charlie and I strapped ourselves into hard chairs behind him.

"The enabling code for emergency vehicles used to be five-six-seven," he said. "If that doesn't work, we'll have to figure out a way to subvert it." He punched those numbers into a keypad and was rewarded with a chime.

"Destination?" the vehicle asked.

"Manual control," the sheriff said.

"Proceed. Drive carefully."

He put the selector on FORWARD and the electric motor whined, increasing in pitch and volume until all six wheels broke free of the ice with a satisfying crunch. We lurched forward and the sheriff steered the thing cautiously around to the front of the spaceport, and took the road toward town.

The spongy metal tires made a sandpapery sound on the icy road. My watch beeped and we stopped long enough for me to step outside and give Marygay a progress report.

There weren't any suburbs on this side of town; no building was allowed in the direction of the spaceport. Once we passed the five-kilometer limit, though, we were in the city.

It was an interesting part of Centrus. The oldest buildings on the planet were here, squat rammed-earth structures with log framing on the doors and windows. They were dwarfed by the brick buildings of the next generation, two and three stories high.

One of the old houses was standing with its front door open, hanging loose on one hinge. We stopped, and walked over to take a look. I heard the sheriff unsnap his holster. Part of me said *What the hell does he expect to find?* and part of me was reassured.

Dim light came through the dirty windows, revealing a horrible sight: the floor was scattered with bones. The sheriff kicked at a few and then squatted to inspect a pile of them.

He picked up a long one. "These aren't Man or human bones." He tossed it away and stirred the pile. "Dogs and cats."

"With the open door, this was the only shelter for them when winter came," I said.

"And the only source of food," Charlie pointed out. "Each other." We'd brought dogs and cats to this place knowing they'd have to be dependent, parasites, for most of the year. They had been a welcome link to the chain of life that began on Earth.

And ended here? I felt a sudden urgency to get on into town.

"Nothing here for us." The sheriff felt it, too; he stood up abruptly and wiped his hands on the greasy coveralls. "Let's move on."

Interesting that we had instinctively assumed that I was in charge from the time the shuttle left orbit, but now the sheriff was in the driver's seat, figuratively as well as literally.

As the sun rose higher, we drove down Main Street, steering around abandoned vehicles. The road and sidewalks were badly in need of repair. We lurched over a choppy sea of frost heaves.

The cars and floaters were not just abandoned; they were piled up in knots, mostly at intersections. People go off automatic inside the city limits, so when their drivers disappeared, the vehicles just kept going until they ran into something heavy.

Most people's homes were open to the sun. That was not reassuring, either. Who leaves for a long journey without drawing the curtains? The same people who leave their floaters in the middle of the street, I guess.

"Why don't we just stop at random and check a place that's not full of dog bones," Charlie said. He looked like I felt: time to get off this rocking boat.

The sheriff nodded and pulled over to the curb, in case of a sudden onrush of traffic. We got out and went into the closest building, a three-story apartment cluster, armed with our big screwdrivers, to pry open locks.

The first apartment on the right was unlocked. "Man lived here," the sheriff said, betraying some emotion. Most of them didn't need to lock their homes.

It was functional and plain past austerity. A few pieces of wooden furniture without cushions. In one room, five plank beds with the wooden blocks they use for pillows.

I wondered, not for the first time, whether they had pillows stashed somewhere for sex. Those planks would be hard on knees and backs. And did the other one and a half couples watch while a couple was coupling? Adults always lived together in groups of five, while children lived in a supervised creche.

Maybe they all had sex together, every third day. They didn't differentiate between home and het.

The place was completely devoid of ornament, like a Tauran cell. Art belonged in public places, for the edification of all. They didn't keep souvenirs or collect things.

There was a uniform layer of dust on every horizontal surface, and Charlie and I both sneezed. The sheriff evidently lacked that gene.

"We might be able to tell more from a human place," I said. "More disorder, more clues."

"Of course," the sheriff said. "Any other one, I'm sure." The population of Men was spread uniformly through the city, a magnanimous gesture.

The one next door was locked, and so were the other seven on the floor. We didn't have any luck with the screwdrivers.

"You could shoot the lock off," Charlie said.

"That's not safe. And I only have twenty cartridges."

"Somehow," I said, "I think you'll find boxes and boxes of them at the police station."

"Let's go outside and break a window," he said. We went out to the ruined street and he picked up a fist-sized piece of it. He had a pretty good fastball for someone who'd probably never played the game. It starred the glass but bounced back. Charlie and I did the same. After a few repeats, the window was almost opaque with a craze of cracks, but it still held.

"Well . . ." The sheriff extracted his pistol, pointed it at the center of the window, and fired. The noise was astonishingly loud, and echoed wavering down the street. The bullet left a hand-sized hole in the ruined glass. He aimed a meter to the right and fired again, and most of the window collapsed in a satisfying cascade.

It was time to make contact again, so we rested for a few minutes while I gave Marygay a summary of our disturbing observations. We agreed that they should put off landing until we knew a little more. Besides, the last people to be revived were still a little bit weak for the stress of landing.

We didn't have to clear away the glass fragments that still clung to the bottom of the frame. I could reach through and unlatch the window, and it swung out to make a large, if inconvenient, portal. The sheriff and Charlie sort of heaved me through it, and then we pushed and pulled until we were all inside. Then I realized I could have gone around and unlocked the door.

The place had been a mess even before we started shooting it up. City folks. There were piles of books all around the room, most of them with bindings from the university library, now eight MF years overdue.

I checked a diploma on the wall and was mildly surprised—the woman who lived here, Roberta More, was a mathematical physicist who had come out to Paxton to talk to a couple of my students about doing graduate work in Centrus. The four of us had had lunch together.

"Small world," Charlie said, but the sheriff pointed out that it wasn't all that unlikely that one of us would know a random resident here, since we both taught and this was a university neighborhood. I could have argued with his logic, but over the years have learned to find more pleasant ways to waste my time.

Dust and cobwebs everywhere. Four large oil paintings on the wall, not very good to my eye. One, improved by an off-center bullet hole, was signed "To Aunt Rob with love," which probably explained all four.

The chaos in the room seemed natural. Subtract the dust and cobwebs and it would be the typical lair of an academic who lived alone.

It looked like she had been in the kitchen when whatever happened, happened. There was a small wooden dining table with two chairs, one of them piled high with books and journals.

One plate with unidentifiable remains, which was, perhaps, a clue. The kitchen was otherwise neat, in contrast to her working room; all the dishes but that one cleaned and put away. In the center of her table, a porcelain vase with a few brown fragile sticks. Whatever it was, happened in the middle of a meal, and she didn't have time or inclination to finish or clean up. No abandoned clothes, but a person living alone doesn't have to dress for dinner.

Her clothes were laid out on the bed, which was neatly made, its coverlet rich burgundy under the dust. Two paintings by the same artist faced each other from the exact centers of opposite walls. A dresser had three drawers: blouses, pants, and underwear, all precisely folded and stacked. There were two empty suitcases in the closet.

"Well, she didn't pack," Charlie said.

"Didn't have time to. Let me check something." I went back into the kitchen and found the fork she'd been eating with, on the floor to the right of the chair.

"Look at this." I held up the fork, which had a twist of dried something in its tines. "I don't think she had any warning at all. She just plain disappeared, in mid-bite."

"Our antimatter didn't," the sheriff pointed out. "If we're still thinking about a common cause."

"You're the physicist," Charlie said. "What makes stuff disappear?"

"Collapsars. But they reappear somewhere else." I shook my head. "Things *don't* disappear. They might appear to, but they've only changed state or position. A particle and an antiparticle destroy each other, but they're still 'there' in the photons produced. Even things swept up by a naked singularity don't actually disappear."

"Perhaps it was staged, for our benefit," the sheriff said.

"What? Why?"

"I don't have any idea *why*. But it seems to be the only explanation that's physically possible. There would have been ample time to set it up."

"Let's play a joke on those renegades," Charlie said with a broad Centrus accent. "Everybody make it look like you disappeared on 14 Galileo 128; leave your clothing and then tiptoe away naked. Meanwhile, we'll suck the antimatter out of the *Time Warp* and force them to come back."

"And then jump out from wherever they're hiding."

The sheriff was annoyed. "I'm not saying it's *reasonable*. I'm just saying that so far nothing else fits the evidence."

"So let's find some more evidence." I gestured. "Shall we leave by the window, or the door?"

twenty-one

I talked to Marygay a half-dozen times before nightfall. They'd been taking shifts on the binoculars, and hadn't seen any sign of life other than the tracks we made in the snow. They were barely visible to the best observers, though, who knew what they were looking for; the binoculars were only 15 power. So in theory, there could be thousands of people holed up somewhere.

But that hardly seemed possible, in light of what we'd found and hadn't found. Everything pointed to the same impossibility: at 12:28 in the afternoon on 14 Galileo 128, every human, Man, and Tauran disappeared into thin air.

The time was a supposition based on one datum: a broken mechanical clock on the floor of a man's workshop that was full of such curiosities. His clothes were right by the broken clock.

It was starting to get dark as we neared City Center, so we

decided to put that off until we had a full day of light. We were all dog-tired, too, and had only managed to keep our eyes open long enough to have a supper of random boxed goods washed down with melted snow. There'd been a cabinet of wine in Roberta's kitchen, but we were reluctant to take any, stealing from the vanished.

Charlie and I collapsed on the gurneys, or operating tables, in the back of the vehicle, even finding some blow-up pillows. The sheriff slept on the floor, the back of his head resting on a wooden block he'd found on the street.

He got up at dawn, evidently cold, and woke the two of us by turning on the heater. We spent a few groggy minutes regretting the lack of tea or coffee to go with our cold smoked fish and goldfruit. We could break into a house or store to find utensils and tea, and then conjure up a fire somehow. It would have been easy in Paxton, where every house had a practical fireplace. In Centrus it was all central heating and air pollution laws.

I had a sudden desire to go back to Paxton, partly curiosity and partly the irrational hope that this sinister disaster hadn't spread that far; that my home would be the same place I'd left two months or twenty-four years ago. That Bill would be there, repentant but otherwise unchanged.

We saw the trio of ships drift overhead from the west, dim gold stars in the twilight. I turned on the radio but didn't broadcast, and they were silent, evidently still asleep.

I hoped. Anything could happen, here, now.

The sheriff wanted to go to the police station first. That was the only building in Centrus that he really knew, and if there had been any premonition of disaster at the official level, we might find evidence there. We had no objection. I wanted most to go to the communications center, where there was a line to Earth, but that could wait.

The station is half the Law Building, a four-story mirror monolith. The east half comprises the courts; the west, the cops. We went around to the west door and walked in.

Inside, it was pretty dark, and we paused for a minute to let our eyes become accustomed to it. The window wall was at minimum polarization, but it still let in only a thin grey fraction of the morning light.

The security gate stayed open in spite of the sheriff's pistol and our potentially lethal screwdrivers. We walked up to the front desk and I turned the log around and flashed it with my penlight.

"Twelve twenty-five, it says. Parking violation." Civilian clothes and shoes in front of the desk, a sergeant's uniform behind. He was probably arguing about the ticket at 12:28. The sergeant wanting him to disappear so he could go to lunch. Well, he got half his wish.

The sheriff led us across to the other side of the large room, past dozens of office cubicles, some plain grey or green boxes, others decorated with pictures and holos. In one, an exuberant spray of artificial flowers caught the beginning of the day's light.

We went to the briefing room, where all the officers would gather in the morning, to review the day's plans. If the board said "12:28—DUMP CLOTHES AND GET ON BUS," at least part of the mystery would be cleared up.

The briefing room was about sixty folding chairs that had started out in orderly lines, facing a wipe-board on which the writing was still clear. It was mostly code, which the sheriff identified as case numbers and squads. The message "Birthdays today: Lockney and Newsome" probably had no hidden significance.

We went off in search of cartridges for the pistol, but in most of the little carrels there were either no weapons or more modern ones, worthless without power. Finally we found a supply room with a half-open divided door—I asked whether they still called them Dutch doors; and the sheriff said no, *range* doors, for whatever reason. (I've always had trouble with the language because there are so many words identical to English ones, but unrelated except for sound.)

They had more ammunition there than you could cart away with a wheelbarrow. Charlie and I each took a heavy box, though I wondered what in the world he planned to shoot with it.

He took four boxes, and as we carried them back to the ambulance, provided an oblique answer. "You know," he said, "this looks like the result of some ideal weapon. Kills all the people and leaves all the things untouched."

"They had one like that back in the twentieth," I said. "The neutron bomb."

"It made their bodies disappear?"

"No, you had to take care of that part yourself. Actually, I guess it would preserve bodies for a while, by irradiating them. It was never used."

"Really? You'd think every police department would have one."

Charlie laughed. "It would simplify things. They were designed to kill whole cities."

"Whole cities of humans?" He shook his head. "And you think *we're* strange."

We were back outside in time for Marygay's pass. She said they were going to de-orbit and come in on the next pass, so we wanted some real mass between us and the spaceport.

They'd decided not to wait for the others. Too much weird was going on. Antimatter evaporating was no more or less odd than what we'd been seeing, and we did know it could happen, and strand them up there.

twenty-two

I was sure the landing would have an unearthly beauty; I've seen matter/antimatter drives from a safe distance, or somewhat safe. Brighter than the sun, an eerie brilliant purple.

We weren't sure how little shielding would be safe, so at the appointed time we cautiously made our way down into the Law Building's second basement.

The penlight showed orderly boxes of documents and a wall of old law books, from Earth, mostly in English. There was another wall, behind a locked iron gate, with hundreds of wine bottles, some of them with labels as old as forty MF years.

I gave the lock a tug and it clicked open. I pulled us each out three bottles at random. The sheriff protested that he didn't drink wine. I told him I didn't shoot anymore, but I'd carried his damned ammunition.

There was a triple sonic boom, pretty loud even at our

depth, and then a protracted sound like sheets being torn. I ran upstairs as soon as it quit.

Winded by the unaccustomed exercise, I held it down to a dogtrot going through the dead building and out the door.

Standing in the middle of Main Street, I could see the three golden needles of the ships on the horizon.

Marygay was barely understandable through a roar of static from secondary radiation. "Landing went okay," she said. "Some stuff came loose and crashed around."

"How soon can you disembark?" I shouted.

"You don't have to *shout*! Maybe an hour. Don't you come too close before that."

We spent the time loading the ambulance with ninety parkas from the police wardrobe—better too warm than too cold—and I chose a few cases of food from a grocery down the street.

There would be plenty to eat for the next several years—unless everybody else suddenly showed up, naked and hungry. And pissed off. If one kind of magic is possible, or two, counting the antimatter—then what kind of magic might happen tomorrow?

The sheriff seemed to have been thinking along those lines himself. When we finished loading up the clothing and food and a few extra bottles of wine—one for each ten people didn't seem adequate—he said, "We have to talk to Antres 906."

"About what?"

"This. I never could understand Tauran humor. But it would be just like them to demonstrate a new scientific principle with a huge practical joke."

"Sure. Killing off a whole planet."

"We don't know that they're dead. Until we have a body, it's still a 'missing persons' case." I couldn't tell whether he was being ironic, playing cop. Maybe exposure to the big-city police station had done something to him.

In one of the vehicle's many latched drawers, labeled only by number, we found a radiation counter. It didn't need a power source in daylight. I pointed it toward the ships, and the needle gave a little quiver, well below the red sector labeled LEAVE AREA.

"So? Let's go on in."

"Inverse-square law," I said. "We'd probably get fried if we got within half a klick." I was guessing, of course; I didn't know anything about secondary radiation.

I thumbed the radio. "Marygay, have you asked the ship how long it will be until you can disembark?"

"Just a second." I could hear a vague mumble mixed with the static. "It says fifty-eight minutes."

"Okay. We'll meet you there about then." I nodded to Charlie and the sheriff. "Might as well get started, and keep an eye on the counter."

Going back was a lot easier than coming in had been. We wallowed across a ditch and then drove along the level mud that paralleled the broken-up road. We did wait for fifteen minutes at about the two-kilometer mark, watching the needle quiver less and less.

What to do with 90, or 150, people? Food was not a problem, and shelter was just a matter of breaking and entering. Water *was* a problem, though.

The sheriff suggested the university. It had dormitories, and a river ran through the middle of it. There might even be a way to jury-rig electricity, I thought; I remembered seeing a field full of solar collectors just off campus, and wondering what they were for—teaching, research, or maybe a backup power supply.

Our ambulance had just crawled onto the landing field

when the unloading ramp on Marygay's ship rolled down. People wobbled down it carefully, tentatively, in groups of five, which was the capacity of the elevator down from the SA pods and control room.

When she came down in the last group, I let out a held breath and realized how tense I'd been, ever since we'd admitted the possibility that they could have been marooned up there. I went halfway up the ramp and took her in my arms.

The other two ships were emptying out as well, people milling around the ambulance trying on parkas for fit, chattering away with the release of tension and happiness at reunion—it had only been a couple of months, subjective, but that twenty-four years was somehow just as real.

Of course everybody knew what we had found, or not found, on the surface, and they were full of apprehension and questions. I avoided them by taking Marygay off to "confer." After everybody was on the ground and in warm clothes, I went halfway up the ramp and waved both arms for attention.

"We've decided to set up temporary quarters at the university. So far, this ambulance is our only working vehicle; it can take ten or twelve in at a time. Meanwhile, let's all move indoors, out of the wind."

We sent the ten biggest, strongest people first, so they could get to work on breaking into the dormitory rooms, while Charlie and I led the others to the cafeteria where we had found our first planetside meal. They walked silently by the eerie piles of old clothing, which had some of the appearance of bodies felled by a sudden disaster, like Pompeii.

Food, even old boxed fruit, cheered them up. Charlie and I answered questions about what we'd found in the city.

Alysa Bertram asked when we could start planting. I didn't

know anything about that, but a lot of the others did, and there were almost as many opinions as people. None of the ones who'd come from Centrus were farmers; the farmers from Paxton were unfamiliar with the local conventions. It was obvious, though, that it wouldn't just be a matter of picking up where the previous tenants had left off. Farming around here was specialized and technology-intensive. We had to devise ways to break up the soil and get water to it without using electricity.

Lar Po, also no farmer, listened to the arguments and seriously suggested that our best chance for survival was to find a way back to Paxton, where we'd have a fighting chance of growing enough to feed ourselves. It would be a long walk, though.

"There's plenty of time to experiment," I reminded them. "We could probably survive here for a generation, scavenging and living off the ship rations." A few weeks on the ship rations, though, would drive anyone to agriculture. That was undoubtedly part of the plan.

The sheriff came back with the welcome news that they'd found a dormitory on the river that didn't even require breaking into. The rooms had electronic locks, and power failure had opened everything up.

I sent Charlie out to start setting up work details. We had to have a water system and temporary latrine as soon as possible, and then organize into search parties to map out the location of resources in the city.

Marygay and I wanted to go downtown, though, to look for two more pieces to the puzzle. The Office for Interplanetary Communications.

twenty-three

Like the Law Building, the OIC had been unlocked in the middle of the day. The sheriff dropped us off and we walked right in—and were startled to find artificial light inside! The building was independent of the city's power grid, and whatever it used was still working.

Direct broadcasts from Earth wouldn't be useful, since it's 88 light-years away. But messages via collapsar jump only took ten months, and there should be a log somewhere.

There was also Mizar, only three light-years away. Its Tauran planet Tsogot had a Man colony, and we might hear something from them, or at least call them, and hear back six years later.

It wasn't a matter of just picking up a mike and flipping a switch—if it was, you did have to know which mike and which switch. None of the terse labels were in English, of course, and

Marygay and I didn't know much MF other than idiomatic conversation.

We called the sheriff to come back and translate. First he had to pick up a load of food downtown and ferry it to the dorm; then he'd come by on his way to the next pickup.

While we waited, we searched the place pretty thoroughly. There were two consoles in the main large room, with signs that identified them as "incoming" and "outgoing" (though the words are so similar, we might have been exactly wrong about both), and each console was divided into thirds—Earth, Tsogot, and something else, probably "other places." The ones for Tsogot had Tauran resting frames as well as human chairs.

When the sheriff showed up he brought along Mark Talos, who had worked with the phone system in Centrus, and was pretty fluent in Standard.

"They don't pick up everything from Earth all the time," he said. "That would be insane and probably impossible. But there's one frequency they do monitor and record all the time. It's basically an ongoing archive. Important messages come and go by way of the collapsar drone, but this one is basically 'Here's what happened on Earth eighty-eight years ago today.' "

He stepped up to the console and studied it. "Ah, Monitor 1." He flipped a switch and there was a rapid, high-pitched flow of the language they call Standard.

"So the one under it is Monitor 2?"

"Not exactly. More like '1A'." He turned off the first one and clicked on 1A. Nothing. "I'd guess that it talks to the collapsar drone, and maybe to people who go back and forth. That might be done at the spaceport, though."

"Can we send a message to Earth?" Marygay asked.

"Sure. But you'll be . . . we'll all be pretty old by the time it gets there." He waved at the chair. "Just sit down and push the red button in front, the one that says HIN/HAN. Then press it again when you're done."

"Let me write down the message first." She took my hand. "We'll all take a look at it and make sure it has everything."

"They're probably getting pretty curious," Mark said.

"Oh, yeah?" I said. "Where are they, then?" I looked at the sheriff. "Are humans that unimportant in the scheme of things? That we could suddenly disappear, and they don't even bother to send a ship to check?"

"Well, they'd still be getting radio from—"

"Eighty-eight years ago, but bullshit! Don't they think that twenty-four years without an urgent message, via collapsar jump, might be cause for concern? We send several a year."

"I can't speak for them—"

"I thought you were a group fucking *mind!*"

"William . . ." Marygay said.

The sheriff's mouth was set in a familiar line. "We don't know that they haven't responded. If they came and found what we have found, they wouldn't necessarily stay. Why *would* they stay? We weren't due back for another forty thousand years."

"That's true, sorry." It still bothered me. "But they wouldn't come all the way here, take a look around, and go back without leaving a sign."

"We don't know they haven't left a sign," Marygay said. "It would probably be out at the spaceport."

"Or maybe here."

"If so, it's not obvious," Mark said. He stepped to the next station. "Want to try Tsogot?"

"Yeah, let's do it while the sheriff's here. He knows more Tauran than we do."

He clicked a few switches and shook his head. Turned a dial up and the room filled with a roar of white noise.

"That's all they're sending," he said.

"A dead line?" I asked, suspecting the answer.

"Nothing wrong with the circuit," he said slowly. "Just an open mike at the other end."

"So the same thing happened there," the sheriff said, and corrected himself: "*May* have happened."

"Is it continuously recorded?" I asked.

"Yeah. If it stops 3.1 years after the big day, then it's compelling evidence. I can check that out." He turned off the white noise and fiddled with some dials. He slid a Tauran keyboard out of the way and a human one took its place.

"Think I can make it go fast-forward here." A small screen gave him date and time, about eight years ago, and he turned the sound back up. Tauran chatter got faster and faster, more high-pitched, and then suddenly stopped. "Yep. Same time, about."

"There and here and where else?" I said. "Maybe Earth didn't send anybody here because there's nobody *there*."

twenty-four

The next week was too busy with practical matters to allow much time or energy for mystery. We were keeping the same leadership until things settled down, so I was pretty occupied with the business of turning this corner of a ghost town into a functional town.

People wanted to roll up their sleeves and get the farms started, but our immediate needs were power, water, and sanitation. Another vehicle or two wouldn't hurt, either, but nothing turned up in the first search.

The solar power plant the university maintained outside of the city limits was evidently for teaching, thank goodness, rather than research. It wasn't working, but that was because it hadn't been completely reassembled for the nth generation of engineering students. I took a mechanic and an engineer out there, and after we found the plans, it only took us a day to reconstruct it and two days to carefully take it apart.

Then we moved the pieces to the dormitory and reassembled it on the roof, and started charging fuel cells. People weren't too happy about all of the electricity going into batteries when it could be giving them light and heat, but first things first. (My mother and father were always talking about "power to the people." A good thing they weren't here to agitate.)

We got two delivery vans running—I guess we should have called them "scavenger" vans—and raided a plumbing supply depot and a hardware store for the things we needed to get running water in the dorm. We basically pumped water from the river, presumably clean, up to a collapsible swimming pool on the roof, which served as a holding tank. That gave us gravity-fed plumbing for the kitchen and the dormitory's first floor, complete with hot water, since it was only a matter of finding the right adapters to run the water through a heater. Still no toilets, since the dorm used conventional "flash and ash" disposal, completely sanitary but requiring truly huge amounts of power. There wasn't enough water to convert to the ancient kind of plumbing I grew up with, and I don't know what you could safely do with the effluent anyhow. I remember big sewage plants, but I'm not sure how they did what they did. So we kept using slit latrines, a simple design from an army manual, and Sage was researching for more permanent solutions.

The fourth ship, Number Two, came into orbit after twelve days and landed without incident. Its passengers all got second-floor rooms, except for Cat. Ami Larson really needed someone sympathetic; she was grieving over Teresa and feeling guilty for having abandoned her and their daughter. Cat had been het since she came to Middle Finger, but she'd been lesbian all her life before that. Which was probably less important than having twenty years' more experience than Ami, in love and loss, and a patient ear.

So she was next door, which shouldn't have bothered me—would it have, if Cat had been an old *boy*friend? Maybe it was the long period of their lives (only about a year in real time) that was theirs alone, which I could never share—when I had been out of the picture, presumed dead.

Of course all of us first-generation veterans who'd been home had been switched to het, as a condition for coming to Middle Finger and jumping in the gene pool. Teresa showed how effective that was. And I knew Charlie had had at least one fling with a guy, maybe for old time's sake. Boys will be girls and girls will be boys, we used to say, in my unenlightened youth.

Mark kept searching for more information at the OIC, but had found nothing new. He also spent days prowling around the spaceport, but in neither place was there any record of collapsar-jump messages from Earth, either before or after the disaster. They were evidently kept secret from hoi polloi; the sheriff had no idea where they might be. Of course, even if we did find messages and there were none from Earth after the Day plus ten months, it wouldn't prove anything. There wasn't anyone here to receive.

(In fact, we could be getting messages from Earth every hour, via collapsar, and never know it. The transmitter comes tearing out at a velocity much higher than Mizar's escape velocity, since the small collapsar's in a tight orbit around Mizar. It whips by MF at fifty or a hundred times the planet's escape velocity, and sends its message down in a burst, and goes off for parts unknown. It's only about the size of a fist, so it's almost undetectable if you don't know the frequency it's using.)

People were excited about an expedition to Earth. The escape ships still had plenty of fuel for a collapsar jump, there and back. If there were still people and Man and Tauran on Earth, they might be able to help us figure out what had happened. If there were none, we'd be no worse off; one more bit of data.

Or so the reasoning went. I agreed, but some were not so sure that we had so completely cut our bonds to Earth. If everyone was gone, if they'd disappeared on the Day, we wouldn't stop hearing from them for another sixty-four Earth years. By that time, we'd be re-established on MF—it would be a shock, but life would go on.

If we were to find out now, still reeling from the original disaster, that we were alone in the universe—and still vulnerable to whatever force had snuffed out everyone else—it might be more than we could handle, as individuals and as a culture. So the theory went.

We were not too stable "as a culture" even now. If the last ship was indeed lost, we totaled 90 people, only 4 of them children. (Two of the 9 who died in SA were under twelve years of age.) We had to start making babies, wholesale as well as retail, hatching some of the thousands of ova frozen aboard the ships.

The prospect was not greeted with enthusiasm. A lot of the people were like me and Marygay: we've already *done* that! Among the various options we'd seen opening up in middle age—like the wild scheme to highjack the *Time Warp*—starting a second family was pretty low on the list.

Sara comprised one-fourth of the females old and young enough for natural motherhood, and she wouldn't have felt ready for it even if any of the available men appealed to her. None of them did.

The sheriff suggested we raise a large batch Man-style, in a group creche, with no parents as such, just supervisors. I could see some merit to it, since a large majority of them actually wouldn't have living parents, and if it wasn't for the association with Man, I think most would have gone along with it. But there was a general counter-sentiment; this was the kind of thing we wanted to *escape* from, and now you want to re-invent it?

They might reconsider when they have four or five infants crawling around. The council decided on a compromise, only possible because we had people like Rubi and Roberta, who were mad about children but unable to have their own. They volunteered to supervise a creche. Every year—three times a Year— they would hatch eight or ten from the ship's stores; they'd also take on the stewardship of unwanted children born the old-fashioned way.

Antres 906 was probably worse off than any of us, though of course it's hard to say anything about a Tauran's emotional state. For all it knew, Antres 906 was the last survivor of its race. They didn't have gender, but they couldn't reproduce without an exchange of genetic material—a holdover from their ancient past, since for millenniums all Taurans had been genetically identical.

People were getting used to the sight of it wandering around, trying to be helpful, but it was like the situation aboard the *Time Warp*: it essentially had no useful skill, being a linguist who was the sole speaker of its language, and a diplomat representing only itself.

Like the sheriff, the Tauran could tap into the Tree, but they both had the same experience. There was no sense of any danger or even problem approaching, but after the Day, no information had been added. The last collapsar-jump message from Earth, three weeks before the Day, also had no premonitions of disaster, from either Man or Tauran.

Antres 906 was in favor of going to Earth or Kysos, nominally the Tauran home planet, and volunteered to make the collapsar jump alone, and come back with a report. Marygay and I believed it was sincere, and I think we knew Antres 906 better than anyone but the sheriff. But most people thought that would be the last we saw of ship or Tauran (but some of them thought it would be worth losing a ship to get rid of the last surviving enemy).

A lot of people did want to go check out Earth, with or without Antres 906. We left a sheet on the dining room bulletin board, and got thirty-two volunteers.

Including Marygay and Sara and me.

Logic would dictate that the ones least essential to the fledgling colony ought to go. But it was hard to say who was more valuable than who, beyond a few who couldn't be replaced, like Rubi and Roberta (who weren't on the list anyhow), and Diana and two young people she was training to be doctors (who were).

The council decided that twelve would be selected from a pool we winnowed to twenty-five non-essentials. (I got disappointingly little argument when I insisted I was not essential.) The sheriff and Antres 906 would go, as observers with unique points of view.

But the fourteen wouldn't leave before deep winter, when not much work would be done, anyhow. The expedition could go to Earth, look around, and be back before spring.

When to make the choice? Stephen and Sage, both on the list, wanted to go ahead and get it over with. I argued for waiting until the last minute, ostensibly to make it more of an occasion; give people a little bit of drama that didn't have to do with day-to-day survival. Actually, my motivation was purely statistical—given a year and a half, some of the twenty-five were bound to change their minds, or die, or otherwise become ineligible, thus increasing our chances.

Marygay and I had decided we would only go if both of us were chosen. If Sara were chosen, she would go, period. She was apologetic about that, but adamant, and I was secretly proud of her for her independence, if apprehensive about the separation.

The council agreed to wait, and we went back to the job of making Centrus livable. The problem of power generation was frustrating and basic. We had always taken free and abundant power for granted: three microwave relay satellites had been in place for more than a century, turning solar power into microwaves and beaming it down. But there's no such thing as a simple stable orbit around MF, not with two large moons and the sun a close double star. Without supervision, the three satellites had wandered off on their own. Eventually, we'd be able to go out and retrieve them, or build and orbit new ones, but for now, our industrial planet was closer to the nineteenth century than the twenty-first. Likewise, any of the three spaceships out on the pad had enough energy to keep us going for decades, but we had no way to release it slowly and safely.

In fact, a vocal minority, led by Paul Greyton, wanted those three ships parked in orbit, right now—before something happened to their magnetic containment apparatus, and we were all instantly vaporized. I understood his concern and didn't entirely disagree, even though the containment fields couldn't possibly fail so long as particle physics worked. Of course, particle physics didn't predict antimatter dwindling away of its own accord, either.

Parking them would require the shuttle, too, and I wouldn't mind the practice. But the rest of the council was unanimous in rejecting Greyton. To most people, the sight of the ships on the horizon was comforting, a symbol of options, possibilities.

W e got two multi-purpose farming vehicles fired up, and I cheerfully delegated authority for *that* little set of problems to Anita Szydhowski, who used to keep the Paxton co-op organized.

There were too many choices. If we had landed on a random earthlike planet, it would be no problem; there were super-hardy varieties of eight basic vegetables in the ships' survival stores. But to get that hardiness, the breeders had to trade off things like taste and yield.

None of the Earth plants on Middle Finger had survived eight hard winters, but there were plenty of seeds in stock, a good fraction of which would be viable—plus hundreds of varieties in cryonic storage at the university. Anita wound up being Solomon-like, making sure enough of the super-hardy were planted to get us through the next year before allotting acreage for the traditional crops, riskier because of the age of the seeds. Then a few acres on the campus itself, for the three ex-farmers who had been itching for years to get their hands on the exotics the university doled out on rare occasion.

I restarted the teaching schedule I'd been following on *Time Warp*—much, of course, to the students' delight. I could drop general science, sadly, since my two youngest students had died in SA, but had to add calculus because the higher-math teacher, Grace Lani, had also died. That was a challenge. Doing calculus is a lot easier than teaching it, and the students I used to have had all been beyond the basics, so I didn't have any experience with the chore.

After a month had passed, we were able to make an expedition to Paxton. This took both vans out of service for two days—their range was about a thousand kilometers, so the van that made the trip had to carry along the other van's fuel cells.

The council magnanimously decided that one of the council should do it, and I drew the short straw. For my assistant and co-driver, I chose Sara. Like almost everyone, she was intensely curious. Also young and strong, to help with driving—all manual, of course—and changing over the heavy fuel cells. Marygay approved, though she would've liked to go herself. Sara was growing away from us, fast, but this was one area where our interests converged.

The van could carry three tonnes, so we could bring back a certain amount of stuff. I had Sara canvass people, and then we sat down with the list and made decisions. It was like the *Time Warp* winnowing process, in miniature. There weren't very many purely sentimental requests, since those things had been taken aboard the time ship and either brought back or abandoned. But there was a limit to the time and effort we could spare—it would be worth going to Diana's office and getting the medical records of the thirty-one of us she'd had as patients, for instance, but I wasn't going to ransack Elena Monet's place to find her crocheting kit.

We did have some hard decisions, juggling time and weight and needs, individual and communal. We were going to load Stan Shank's ceramic kiln, even though it weighed half a tonne and you'd think such things would not be rare. But he'd searched Centrus, and all nine of the kilns he'd found were ruined; left on until they'd burned out.

Sara and I didn't have anything on the list. But there was a little slack.

We left at first light, and a good thing. The trip, normally eight hours, took twenty, most of it crawling along the shoulder of the road rather than trying to negotiate the pavement's rubble.

When we got there, we went straight through town to our old place. Bill had moved in as temporary caretaker, until someone else came along, able and willing to fish in exchange for a nice old house.

We went straight to the kitchen and built a fire. I left Sara to do that while I went out to the lake for a couple of buckets of water, for which I had to break a skin of ice.

In the barrel on the end of the dock, the stasis field was still on; it requires no power to maintain. It was about one-quarter full of fish. I went back to the kitchen for tongs and brought in a few. Absolute zero, of course, but they'd thaw in time for breakfast.

We warmed the water over the fire and drank old wine— I'd bartered it from Harras not five months ago—and when the water was hot enough, I carried a candle into the cold living room to read, while Sara bathed. Having grown up in a nudist commune, and going from there to the army's communal showers, I didn't have any modesty about bathing, and neither did Marygay. So of course our children turned out to be prudes.

It looked like Bill had still been here on the Day, and not alone. I recognized the pile of his clothes where he'd been sitting on the couch in the living room, next to a pile of woman's clothing. Seeing his clothes was a sudden shock; my head swam and I had to grope for a chair.

When I could stand again, feeling curious and obscurely guilty, I checked upstairs, and yes, two people had slept in his unmade bed. I wondered who she was and whether they'd had time, or inclination, to fall in love.

After she'd washed up, Sara looked at her brother's clothes and fell silent. She found us reasonably fresh linen and went upstairs to change her bed and sleep, but for a long time, I could hear, she tossed and turned. I just made a pallet on the floor by the fire, no desire to sleep in our old bedroom alone.

In the morning I broiled the fish in the fireplace, and made a pot of rice that barely seemed a decade old. Then we went out on various errands, a pair of holo cameras mounted in front of the van. Stephen Funk had insisted on that; someday it would be a valuable historic record. And people would be curious about what their homes looked like, abandoned for eight years.

Most of them would be unhappy, since very few had had landscaping of native plants alone. There was status in planting and maintaining Earth stock, but very little of it had survived even one hard winter unattended. The native forms had taken over, especially the large and small green mushrooms, neither plant nor fungus, pretty ugly even out in the woods, where they belonged. All of the lawns were full of it, knee high to head high. The town looked like a nightmarish fairy tale.

We gathered records and artifacts and a few specialized tools—Stan's kiln, as he'd said, disassembled into ten pieces, but it was still a monster to load. By the end of the day, we were tired and depressed and ready to leave. But we had to wait till dawn.

I made a stew of boxed fruit with rice, and we sat by the fire, eating and drinking too much.

"Earth is going to be like this to you, isn't it?" Sara said. "Only worse."

"I don't know," I said; "it's been so long. I think I've adjusted to the fact that there won't be much I recognize."

I added some wood to the fire and went back to refill the wine pitcher. "I guess I told you about the guy from the 22nd."

"A long time ago. I forget."

"He came to Stargate while I was waiting for Charlie and Diana and Anita to get hetero-ed. He was alone, supposedly the only survivor of some battle. Too vague about it, though."

"You assumed he'd deserted."

"Right. But that wasn't what interested me." The wine was cool and tangy. "He'd been back to Earth in the twenty-fourth. Born in 2102, he'd mustered out into the 2300's. Like your mother and me, he couldn't tolerate what passed for Earth society, and re-upped to get away from it.

"But what he described sounded so much better than the world he'd been born into. That was a half-century after Marygay and I had left, and it was even worse. The leading cause of death in the United States was murder, and most of the murders were legal duels. People settled arguments and even made business deals and *gambled* with weapons—I put up everything I own, and you put up everything you own, and we fight to the death for the whole pile."

"And he liked that."

"He *loved* it! And after all his commando training and combat experience, he was looking forward to becoming a wealthy man.

"But the Earth wasn't like that anymore. There was a warrior class, and you were born into it, biologically engineered. They went into the army as children, and never left it; never mixed with polite society—and I mean *polite*. The Earth had become a planet of docile lambs who lived communally; no one owned— or desired—more than anyone else had; no one even spoke ill of anyone else.

"They even *knew* that their harmony was artificial, imposed by biological and social engineering, and were glad for it. The fact that a horrific war was being waged on a hundred planets, in their name, just made it the more logical that their own daily lives be serene and civilized."

"So he ran back to the army?"

"Not immediately. He knew how lucky he'd been to survive, and wasn't eager to press his luck. He couldn't live with the sheep, so he took off on his own—wandering through the countryside, trying to live off the land.

"But they wouldn't let him! They wouldn't leave him alone. They could always find him, and every day they sent someone new to try to bring him into the fold. He'd fight the messengers—or at least assault them; they didn't fight back—and even killed some. A new one would show up the next day, full of pity and concern.

"After a month or two, the one who showed up was an army re-enlistment officer. He was gone the next day."

We watched the fire for a while. "You think you could've adjusted?"

"Not adjusted. I could never be like them. But I could have lived in their world."

"So could I," she said. "It sounds like Man's world."

"Yeah, I suppose it does." The one I rejected for Middle Finger. "It was probably a first step. Even though we didn't make peace with the Taurans for another thousand years."

She took our bowls and spoons to the sink, walking with careful unsteadiness. "I sort of hope it's different, if I get, if we get chosen."

"It will be. Everything changes." I wasn't sure, though, once Man got ahold of it. Why mess with perfection?

She agreed, and made her way upstairs to bed. I washed the bowls and spoons, pointlessly. This house probably wouldn't have inhabitants again in my lifetime.

I made up my pallet by the fire, after wrestling a big over-night log into place. I lay down and stared at the flames, but couldn't fall asleep. Maybe I'd had too much wine; that some-times happens.

For some reason I was haunted by images of war—not only actual memories of the campaigns and the gore we twice had to deal with in transit. But I also went way back to training; to the ALSC-induced fantasies of combat, killing phantoms with every-thing from a rock to a nova bomb. I thought about having some more wine, enough to chase them away. But I'd be driving, steer-ing, at least half of a long day.

Sara clumped down sniffling with her pillow and blankets and said, "Cold." She snugged up to me the way she used to when she was little, and in a minute was softly snoring. The familiar warm smell of her drove the demons away, and I slept, too.

twenty-six

E ventually, other people went on expeditions to Thornhill,
     Lakeland, and Black Beach/White Beach, scavenging
from the lost past. No new clues as to what had happened
showed up, but the dorm did become more homey, and
crowded, with the junk they brought back.

Toward the end of spring, we began to expand, although it
was more like an amoeba slowly splitting. There were no central
utilities, and wouldn't be for some time, so they had to reproduce in miniature our mechanisms for power and plumbing and
so forth.

Nine people moved into a building downtown that had
been called "The Muses," a place where artists, musicians, and
writers lived together. All the materials for those pursuits were
still in place, though the cold had ruined some of them.

Eloi Casi's lover, Brenda Desoi, brought along the unfinished small sculpture that Eloi had given her before we left the *Time Warp*; she wanted to make an installation around it, and she knew that Eloi had spent a deep winter studying and working at The Muses when he was young. She found eight others who wanted to move there and start making art and music again.

There was no objection—in fact, most of us would have borne Brenda out on our shoulders, just to get rid of her. We'd found a storage room full of solar panels and equipment out at the spaceport, and so that was not a problem; Etta Berenger set it up in a few afternoons. She also designed a year-round latrine for them, in an elegant atrium, but allowed them to do the artistic pick-and-shovel work themselves.

That freed up six rooms at the dorm. We shuffled people around so that the west end of the building was given over to Rubi and Roberta's creche and the families who were raising children on their own. It was good for the kids to have other kids around, and marvelous to have a door—the firedoor that isolated the west wing—beyond which children could not go unescorted.

Etta and Charlie and I, along with specialists we'd call in now and then, spent a few hours every afternoon working on plans to reclaim Centrus. We could start out with small colonies like The Muses, but eventually we wanted to have an actual city to grow into.

It would have been easier on Earth, or some other well-behaved planet. Dealing with month after month of bitter cold complicated everything. Just keeping buildings livable was a challenge. In Paxton, we'd supplemented electrical heat with fireplaces and stoves, but out there we had heat farms; fast-growing trees whose limbs were trimmed every year for fuel. Centrus was surrounded by hills with native trees, but their spongy "wood" didn't burn well, and if we cut them down in quantity, we'd cause erosion and probably flooding, during the spring thaw.

The ultimate solution was going to be finding one of those powersats and bringing it back. But that wouldn't be this winter. And this winter had to be dealt with soon—not only did it cool off quickly as the summer faded, but the output of the solar power plant plunged at the same time—we weren't just dealing with the inverse-square law (when the sun became twice as far away, we'd have one-fourth the power), but also more and more cloudy days, lacking weather-control satellites.

So we would go for wood stoves. There was enough wood at Lakeland to keep us warm through dozens of winters. Normally, the heat-farm trees were kept "topped," so they never grew above eye level. Eight uncontrolled seasons had turned those acres into a tall dense jungle of fuel.

In a shed next to a chemical factory outside of Centrus, we found hundreds of steel drums, 100- and 250-liter, which made ideal stoves for heating. I used to be a welder, and in an hour I taught a couple of guys how to cut the proper holes in the drums. Alysa Bertram also knew how to weld; she and I attached the metal ducts to the stoves. Back at the dorm, and at Muses, people were improvising exhaust ducts through windows or walls.

We diverted one farm machine and one van to a wood-gathering detail; it was going to require 850 cords of wood, to be on the safe side. They needed it to make water out of ice, as well as for keeping warm and cooking.

Everybody breathed a little easier when the first crops started coming in. The flock of chickens had grown to laying size. The artists took two pair, which was going to make living in The Muses interesting, come winter. At the dorm, we were able to turn the downstairs cube room into a chicken coop. People who *had* to have a large cube or screen for their movies could share them with the chickens. There weren't going to be regular cube broadcasts for a while, I thought. (That would prove wrong; faced with a long winter's boredom, people would watch anything, even if it was their own neighbors being themselves in front of a camera downstairs.)

The sunny upstairs exercise room became a greenhouse, for growing seedlings to be transplanted. We could also grow greens there during the winter, for which Anita installed three woodstoves and supplemental lighting.

As for the truly *big* winter problem—finding an alternative to running through the snow to bare your butt over a slit trench at fifty below—Sage came up with a solution more direct than elegant. Even at this latitude there was a permafrost layer. Anything below seven meters (and not so deep that the earth began to warm) would freeze and stay frozen forever. We didn't have earthmoving tools, or power, for that matter, to actually dig a pit deep enough and large enough for a population that was ninety and growing. But there was a copper mine only ten klicks out of town, and from it she appropriated shaped charges and a mining laser that did the job.

The folks in town would have to make do with their slit trench, but art always requires sacrifices. Going out to the frozen atrium would put them in touch with nature, and their inner selves.

twenty-seven

worked as hard on the reclamation project as I ever had on anything, outside of combat, and so did Marygay. There was a lot of desperation in the air. We didn't talk about the Earth expedition, not until the day of the drawing.

Everybody gathered at the dorm cafeteria at noon, where there was a glass bowl with thirty-two slips of paper in it. The youngest child who was not too young to be able, Mori Dartmouth, sat up on the table and picked out twelve names for me to announce. Sara was second, and she rewarded me with a squeal of delight. Cat was third, and hugged Sara. Marygay was eighth and she just nodded.

After twelve, my name was still in the bowl. I didn't want to look at Marygay. A lot of other people did. She cleared her throat, but it was Peek Maran who spoke: "Marygay," he said, "you're not going without William, and I'm not going without Norm. It looks like we have a game situation."

"What do you propose?" she said. "We don't have coins."

"No," he said, momentarily puzzled at the word—he was third-generation and had never seen money in any non-electronic form. "Let's empty out the bowl and put our names—no, William's and Norm's—into it. Then have Mori draw." Mori smiled and clapped.

So I won, or we did, and there was a quiet pressure of jealousy in the room. A lot of people who hadn't volunteered their names for the bowl back in the spring would be only too glad to take their chances, and a little trip, now that deep winter loomed.

The physical preparations had been finished months before. We were taking ship Number Two, christened *Mercury*. All of the terraforming and recolonization tools and materials had been taken out; if Earth was deserted, we would just come back with that news, and let later generations decide about repopulating it.

We were prepared for other contingencies, though. Each ship had a fighting suit, and we took all four. We also carried a stasis dome, but elected not to bother with a nova bomb, or any such dramatic weapon. If anything that serious happened, we'd be meat anyhow.

They weren't great fighting suits, since they had to accommodate a range of sizes and skills, and we discussed leaving them behind, as a matter of principle. I argued that we could decide not to *use* them, when the time came, as a matter of principle. But meanwhile, as the poet said, do not go gentle into that bad night. Or something.

book five

THE BOOK OF
APOCRYPHA

twenty-eight

Some Indian tribe or tribes had no ritual for good-byes; the person leaving just turned his back and left. Sensible people. We spent a day making the rounds, saying good-bye to everyone because you didn't dare leave anyone out.

I saw half the people in the colony, anyhow, as mayor, since everybody seemed to be in charge of this or that, and had to come by and give me a report and sketch out what they'd be doing while I was gone. Sage, who would be interim mayor, sat beside me for all of the discussions.

It was also her job, the next day, to make sure everyone was safely underground, away from the launch's radiation, when Marygay pressed the button. Precisely at noon she radioed that everyone but her was downstairs. The button gave her a minute; the ship counted down the last twenty seconds of it.

It was a crushing four gees at first; then two. Then we

floated in free fall for half an orbit, and the ship drove toward Mizar's collapsar at a steady one gee.

A day and a half of constant acceleration. We made simple meals and small talk while Mizar drew closer—finally, closer than you'd like to be, to a young blue star.

The collapsar was a black pinprick against the filtered image of the huge star, and then a dot, and then a rapidly swelling ball, and then there was the odd twisting feeling and we were suddenly in dark deep space.

Now five months to Earth. We got into our coffins—Sara clumsily quick in her modesty about nakedness—and hooked up the orthotics and waited for sleep. I could hear the ship whispering, telling a couple of people to redo this or that attachment, and then the universe squeezed to a pinpoint and disappeared, and I was back in the cool dream of suspended animation.

I'd talked with Diana about the emotional, or existential, discomfort I'd gone through last time, and she said that as far as she knew, there was no medical solution for it. How could there be, when you're metabolizing slower than a sequoia? Just try to think comfortable thoughts before you go under.

It sort of worked. Most of us could see the overhead viewscreen, and I'd set up a program for it to show a sequence of soothing pictures while we waited to cool down. Expressionist paintings, quiet nature photographs. I wondered whether Earth *had* any nature left. Neither Man nor Tauran was sentimental about such things; they found beauty in abstractions.

Well, we didn't have such a great track record, either. Most of human history had been industry *versus* nature, with industry winning.

So I spent the dreaming five months, which sometimes felt

like five minutes, in a series of quiet pastoral environments, most of which were extrapolations of places I'd only read about or seen in pictures; even the commune where I grew up was in a suburb. I had played in neatly manicured parks and dreamed they were jungles. I came back to those dreams now.

It was curious. My dreams didn't take me back to Middle Finger, where Mother Nature and I had always been on intimate, battling terms. No rest in that, I guess.

Coming out of SA was more difficult, and uncomfortable, than when I'd had Diana to help. I was confused and numb. My fingers didn't want to work, and they couldn't tell clockwise from counterclockwise, unscrewing the bypass orthotics. When I lifted myself out I was streaked with blood from the abdomen down, though there was no injury.

I went to help Marygay, and she was only one step behind me, trying to sort out and loosen straps. She had managed not to splash blood all over herself. We both got dressed, and she went back to check on Sara, while I looked at the others.

Then I checked on Rii Highcloud, who was our volunteer medico. She was actually a librarian, way back in real life, but Diana had given her an intense week of training in how to use the standard medical kit aboard the ship.

Antres 906 was alert, and nodded at me when I peered over the edge of the box. Good thing. If something went wrong, the creature would have been at the mercy of a first-aid manual that had an appendix about Taurans.

Jacob Pierson was frozen solid, with no life signs. He had probably been dead for five months. It made me feel vaguely guilty that I didn't like him and hadn't looked forward to working with him.

Everyone else was at least moving. We wouldn't know if they

were well until they were up and talking. Unwellness could take odd forms, too; Charlie had come out of SA on Middle Finger unable to smell flowers, though he could smell other things. (Marygay and I used it as an excuse, a private joke, for not remembering names or numbers: "Must've lost it in SA.")

She said that Sara was coming along fine; she'd needed some mopping up, but didn't want her mother to help, of all people.

We got the screen working, and Earth looked all right, or at least as we expected. About a third of what we could see, between clouds, seemed to be city, a featureless grey, all over northern Africa and southern Europe.

I drank some water and it stayed down, though I could imagine it floating, a cold spherical lump, in my stomach. I was concentrating on that when I realized Marygay was crying, silently, blotting floating tears with her knuckles and forearm.

I thought it was about Pierson and started to say something comforting.

"The same," she said tightly. "Nothing. Just like Middle Finger."

"Maybe they're . . ." I couldn't think of anything. They were dead or gone. All ten billion.

Antres 906 had climbed out of the box and was floating behind me. "This is not unexpected," it said, "since there was no sign of Centrus having been visited by them." It made a strange sound, like a hoarse dove. "I must go to the Whole Tree."

Marygay looked at it for a long moment. "Where is your Tree?"

It cocked its head. "Everywhere, of course. Like a telephone."

"Of course." She unbelted and floated out of the chair.

"Well, let's help people get up and around. See what's down there."

We "buried" Jacob Pierson in space. He was sort of a Muslim, so Mohammed Ten said a few words before Marygay pressed the button that opened the outer lock and spun him gently into the void. It was deferred cremation, actually, since we were in a low enough orbit for him to eventually fall into friction fire.

We landed at Cape Kennedy, far out on a spit, on a special pad reserved for those of us who had to come down in a shower of gamma rays. A personnel carrier, heavily armored, rolled up to wait for us.

After thirty minutes, the radiometer let us exit. The air was sultry warm and heavy with salt fragrance. Wind rushed across mangrove swamps and ruffled our clothing as we walked unsteadily down the gangway. At the bottom, the smell was of burnt metal, and the landing pad patiently ticked as it contracted.

"So quiet," Alysa said.

"This part has always been quiet," Po said, "between launches and landings. I'm afraid the rest of the spaceport is going to be quiet, too. Like ours."

The metal ground still radiated heat. And maybe a few alpha particles. The air was wonderful, though; I was a little giddy from breathing deep.

"Who are you?" the personnel carrier boomed, in Standard. "Where are you from?"

Marygay answered in English. "Speak English. We're just a group of citizens from Middle Finger, a planet of Mizar."

"Here to trade?"

"Just here. Take us to some people."

A double door in the thing's side swung open. "I can take you to the spaceport. I'm not allowed on roads, without wheels."

We entered the thing and four large windows became transparent. Once we were seated, the door closed and the thing backed up, turned around, and lurched toward the other end of the long strip, moving fast. It walked on twelve articulated legs.

"Why don't you have wheels?" I asked, my voice wavering from the carrier's jerky progress.

"I do have wheels. I haven't put them on in a long time."

"Are there any people in the spaceport?" Mohammed asked.

"I don't know. I've never been inside."

"Are there any people in the world?" I asked.

"That is not a question that I am able to answer." It stopped so abruptly that Matt and I, facing forward but not belted in, were almost thrown from our seats. The doors sprung open. "Check to make sure you have all your belongings. Be careful upon exiting. Have a pleasant day."

The spaceport main building was a huge structure with no straight lines; all sweeping parabolas and catenaries, with facets like beaten bright metal. The rising sun gleamed orange from a hundred shiny surfaces.

We walked hesitantly toward the DIIJHA/ARRIVALS door, which for some reason slid open upwards. Walking through it gave me a guillotine kind of anxiety. The others hurried, too.

It wasn't quiet. There was a soothing sound like modulated white noise, pulsing in a rhythm slower than a heartbeat. There were chimes at the edge of perception.

The floor was littered with clothes.

"Well," Po said, "I guess we can turn around and go home."

Antres 906 made a hissing sound I'd never heard, and its left hand tuned in a continual slow circle. "I appreciate your need for humor. But there is much to do, and there may be danger." It turned to Marygay. "Captain, I suggest at least one of you return to the ship for a fighting suit."

"Good idea," she said. "William? Go see if you can catch that thing."

I went back to the arrivals door, which wouldn't open, of course. There was a MOSCH/TRANSPORTATION door a hundred meters away. When I went through it, the carrier minced up, clattering. "I forgot something," I said. "Take me back to the ship."

Putting on fighting suits used to be dramatic and communal. The ready room would have mounting harnesses for as many as forty people; you'd strip and back into the suit, hook up the plumbing and let it clamshell shut around you, and move out. You could have the whole company in suits and, theoretically, outside fighting in a couple of minutes.

When there's no harness and no hardware, and the suit isn't customized for your body, it's neither quick nor dramatic. You squirm this way and that and finally get everything in place, and then try to close it on your own. When it doesn't close, you go back a few steps and start over.

It took almost fifteen minutes. I walked down the gangway, clumsy at first. The carrier doors opened.

"Thanks anyhow," I said. "I think I'll walk."

"That is not allowed," it said. "It is dangerous."

"*I'm* dangerous," I said, and resisted the impulse to tear off a couple of its legs, to see what would happen. Instead, I started running, invoking the suit's strength amplification to give me a broad-jump lope. It wasn't as smooth and automatic as I remembered, but it was fast. I was at the spaceport door in less than a minute.

The door wouldn't open for me, sensing that I was a machine. I walked through it. The shatterproof glass turned opaque, stretched, and ripped apart like cloth.

Marygay laughed. "You could have knocked."

"This is the *way* I knock," I said, amplified voice echoing in the huge hall. I turned it down to conversational volume. "Our odd men out went to find their Trees?" The sheriff and Tauran were missing.

She nodded. "Asked us to wait here. How's the suit?"

"I don't know yet. Leg amplifiers work. Okay on doors."

"Why don't you take it outside and try out the ordnance? It's pretty old."

"Good idea." I went back through the hole I'd made and looked around for targets. What would we not need? I set my sights on a fast-food stand and gave it an order of fries, with the laser finger. It burst into flame in a satisfying way. I flipped a grenade at it and the explosion sort of put out the fire by scattering the pieces.

The personnel carrier came mincing up, accompanied by a small robot with flashing blue lights. It had PARKING POLICE stenciled on front and back.

"You are under arrest," it said, in a huge stentorian voice. "Surrender control to me." That was followed by some almost ultrasonic warbling. "Surrender control to me."

"Sure." I chambered a rocket, which the heads-up thing called MHE. That's not an acronym we used to have. I assumed "medium high explosive" and squeezed it off. It did vaporize the parking robot and leave a crater two meters in diameter, in the process knocking the personnel carrier on its back.

It righted itself by rocking back and forth until it tipped onto its spidery feet. "You didn't have to do that," it said. "You could have explained your situation. You must have a reason for this arbitrary destruction of property."

"Target practice," I said. "This fighting suit is very old, and I had to know how well it works."

"Very well. Are you finished?"

"Not really." I hadn't tried the nukes. "But I'll hold off with the other systems until I have more real estate to work with."

"Real estate outside of Spaceport?"

"Absolutely. There's nothing in here small enough to destroy."

It actually seemed to pause, integrating that statement into its world view. "Very well. I will not call the police again. Unless you destroy something here."

"Scout's honor."

"Please rephrase that."

"I won't hurt anything here without telling you ahead of time."

It sort of threw a mechanical tantrum, stamping its many feet. I supposed it was generating conflicting orders. I left it there to sort things out.

The sheriff came back to the group the same time I did.

"The Whole Tree gives no warning," he said. "There's no sense that anything was going wrong."

"Just like home?" Marygay said.

He nodded. "More complex things are going on," he said, "and the Tree is still trying to make sense of what has happened."

"But it hasn't," Po said.

"Well, now it has new information. What happened to us, out in space, and to Middle Finger. And Tsoget. It may be able to piece something together."

"It thinks by itself?" I said. "Without people connected to it?"

"It's not like thinking, exactly. It just sifts things; makes things more simple for itself. Sometimes the result is like thought."

Antres 906 had returned. "I have nothing to add," it said.

Maybe we *should* have turned around and gone home. Begin to rebuild from what we had. Both the sheriff and the Tauran would have been in favor of that, I think, but we didn't ask them.

"Guess we ought to try a city," Marygay said.

"We're right next door to what used to be the biggest one in the country," Cat said, "at least in terms of acreage."

Marygay cocked her head. "Spaceport?"

"No, I mean *big*. Disney!"

twenty - nine

Marygay and I had been to Disney*world*, as it was still called, in the early twenty-first, and it had been large then. The one we'd gone to was now just one element in a patchwork of "lands"—Waltland, where you visited in groups, and a simulacrum of the place's founder took you around and explained the wonders.

The carrier had amiably agreed to produce wheels, and it got us to the outskirts of Disney in about twenty minutes.

The perimeter of Disney was a huge ring, where parking lots for the patrons alternated with clustered living areas for the people who worked there.

You were supposed to park, evidently, and wait for a Disney bus to take you inside. When we tried to drive through an entrance, a big jolly cartoon robot blocked it off, explaining in a loud kiddy voice that we had to be nice and park like everyone else. It alternated Standard and English. I told it to fuck off, and after that all the machines spoke to us in English.

Goofy was the robot on the third one we tried. I got out in my fighting suit. It said, "Ah-hyuh—what have we here?" and I kicked it over and pulled off its arms and legs and tossed them in four directions. It started repeating "Hyuh . . . that's a good 'un . . . Hyuh . . . that's a good 'un," and I pulled off the meter-wide head and threw it as high and far as I could.

The living areas for the staff were blocked off by holograms that were only partly successful now. On one side we had a jungle where cute baby monkeys played; on the other, a sea of Dalmatian puppies running through a giant's house. But you could see dimly through them, and sometimes they would disappear for a fraction of a second, revealing identical rows of warren housing.

We came out in Westernland, a big dusty old town from a pre-mechanized West that once existed in movies and novels. It wasn't like the spaceport, with clothing scattered all around. It was very neat, and had a sort of dreamlike ordinariness, with people walking about in period costume. They were robots, of course, and their costumes showed unusual fading and wear, plastic knees and elbows showing through frayed holes.

"Maybe the park was closed when it happened," I said, though it would be hard to reconcile that with the thousands of vehicles in ranks and files outside.

"The local time was 13:10 on April 1," the sheriff said. "It was a Wednesday. Is that significant?"

"April Fool's Day," I said. "What a trick."

"Maybe everybody came naked," Marygay suggested.

"I know what happened to the clothes," Cat said. "Watch this." She opened the door and threw out a crumpled piece of paper.

A knee-high Mickey Mouse came rolling out of a trap door in the side of a saloon. It speared the paper with a stick and addressed us, finger wagging, in a scolding squeaky voice: "Less mess! Don't be a pest!"

"We used to throw stuff all around it and get it confused," she said.

The carrier was up on its toes again, to maneuver more easily through the narrow streets, and it tiptoed through this strange land of saloons, dance halls, general stores, and quaint Victorian houses, each with its retinue of shabby busy robots. Where there were wooden boardwalks, the robots had worn a light-colored trail a couple of centimeters deep.

There were broken robots frozen in mid-gesture, and twice we came upon piles of several helpless robots, their legs sawing air, where evidently one had stopped and the others tripped over it. So they weren't true robots, but just mechanical models. Marygay remembered the term "audio-animatronic," and Cat confirmed that two hundred years after we'd been there, the old-fashioned technology had been re-introduced for nostalgia and humor.

One universal anachronism was on the buildings' roofs, with solar cells covering the south side. (A more prosaic anachronism was that every building, even the churches, had something for sale.)

At least it made the business of food and shelter simple. There was enough frozen and irradiated food to last us several lifetimes, most of it more interesting than our survival rations, if less nutritious.

We decided to spend the night at Molly Malone's Wayside Inn. Marygay and I were surprised to see, behind the registration desk, a price list for sexual services. Cat said all you got was robots. Clean robots.

But then our own robot, the carrier, delivered its own larger surprise. We went back out of Molly Malone's to get our bags, and there they were, lined up neatly on the boardwalk.

And behind them, instead of a machine, stood a ruggedly handsome cowboy. He didn't look like the worn-out robots, but he didn't look quite human, either. He was too big, over seven feet tall. He left deep footprints in the dust, and when he stepped onto the boardwalk, it creaked alarmingly.

"I'm not really a carrier," he said. "Not any kind of machine. It was just handy to look and act like one, down at the spaceport."

He talked in a slow drawl that I recognized vaguely from childhood, and then it clicked: he looked like the actor John Wayne. My father had loved his movies and my mother despised him.

While he talked, he rolled a fat joint of tobacco. "I can be the carrier again, or whatever thing or organism we need about that size."

The Tauran spoke up. "Please demonstrate?"

He shrugged and produced a large wooden match, and scratched it alight on the sole of his boot. Sulfur dioxide and, when he puffed the joint into life, the acrid tang of tobacco. I hadn't smelled it in thirty years, or thirteen hundred. Cigarettes, they used to be called.

He stepped back three giant strides and blurred and flowed into the shape of the carrier. But he kept the colors of blue jeans and leather and held the smoldering cigarette in a human hand that grew out of the top.

Then he changed again, into an oversized Tauran, still holding the cigarette. He said something to Antres 906 in rapid Tauran, and then changed back into John Wayne. He took a last puff and pinched the cigarette out between thumb and forefinger.

None of us could come up with anything intelligent to say, so I opted for the obvious: "You're some kind of alien."

"Actually, no; nothing of the kind. I was born on Earth, about nine thousand years ago. It's *you* guys who are creatures from another planet."

"A shape-changer," Marygay whispered.

"Like you're a clothes-changer. To me, I'm always the same shape." He twisted his leg around to a break-bone angle and looked at the boot sole. "You don't have a name for us, but you could call us Omnis. The Omni."

"How many are you?" Po asked.

"How many you need? A hundred, a thousand? I could turn into a troop of Campfire Girls, as long as they didn't mass more than two-some tonnes. Maybe a horde of locusts. But it's hell to get them all back together in one bunch."

"You people have been on Earth for nine thousand years . . ." Max began.

"Try a hundred fifty thousand, and we aren't people. We don't even look like people, most of the time. I was a Rodin sculpture in a museum for more than a century. They never could figure out how the thieves got me through the door." He laughed, and John Wayne split down the middle, and re-formed as two museum guards in uniform, a petite young woman and a fat old man.

They spoke in absolute unison: "When I do something like this, I'm an actual 'group mind,' like Taurans and Man aspire to being. It can be useful, but confusing, too." The two figures collapsed into a pile of hundreds of scuttling cockroaches. Two Mickey Mouse robots rolled toward them, and they quickly re-formed into John Wayne, who kicked one of the robots onto the roof of Molly Malone's.

"How do you do that?" I asked.

"It's a matter of practice. Eye-foot coordination."

"No, I mean how do you change back and forth? You can't take molecules of metal and turn them into organic material."

"I suppose you can," he said. "I do it all the time."

"What I mean is, it's inconsistent with physical law."

"No, it's not. Your version of physics is inconsistent with reality."

I was starting to get an Alice-in-Wonderland dizziness. Maybe Lewis Carroll had been one of them.

"Let me turn it around," he continued. "How do you turn food into flesh? Eating."

I thought for a second. "Your body breaks down the food into simpler compounds. Amino acids, fats, carbohydrates. Components that aren't burned for energy may turn into flesh."

"That's your opinion," he said. "I had a friend a few thousand years ago, not far from here, who said that you took part of the spirit of the animal or plant that you ate, and it became part of your own spirit. Explains all kinds of sickness."

"Very poetic," I said, "but wrong."

"You likewise. You just have different ideas about what poetry is, and what 'right' is."

"Okay. So tell me how you do it."

"I don't have the faintest idea. I was born being able to do it, just as you were born able to metabolize. My Timucuan friend was able to metabolize as well as you, even if he described it differently."

"In nine thousand years, you haven't tried to find out how your body works?"

"Not everybody's a scientist." He changed from John Wayne to a man I vaguely recognized from the kids' schoolwork, an artist whose medium was body sculpture. He had four and six fingers, and a heat-sensing eye installed in his forehead. "I'm a kind of historian."

"You've lived alongside humans since prehistory," Cat said, "and no one ever suspected?"

"We don't keep real good records," he said, "but I think that at first, we were open about what we were, and co-existed. Somewhere along the line, I think when you got language and society, we started to hide out."

"So you became myths," Diane said.

"Yeah; I can do a great werewolf," he said. "And I think we were taken for angels and gods sometimes. Every now and then I'd be a plain human for a lifetime, appearing to age. But that's kind of boring and sad."

"You've been Man as well?" the sheriff asked. "You've tapped into the Tree?"

"Not as tricky as you might think. I have a lot of control over my neural organization. The Tree can't tell me from a human—and you guys *are* just humans, with a hole in your skull and some odd ideas." He turned into Wayne again, and said with the actor's drawl, "Buncha god-damn Commies, if ya ask me."

"Did you do it?" The sheriff and the Omni made an odd tableau in the middle of us: the two biggest men standing there, both with guns holstered on their hips. "Did you make them disappear?"

John Wayne didn't invite him to slap leather, a challenge I don't think he would have understood. He just shook his head sadly. "I don't know what happened. I was in an elevator with two people, two Men, and they just plain disappeared. There was a little 'pop' and their clothes fell to the floor. The elevator doors opened and I rolled out—I was in the shape of a food-dispensing robot—and the whole office building was empty, except for clothes.

"There was a huge racket outside, thousands of traffic accidents. A floater crashed through a picture window; I took human shape and ran down the stairs to the basement until things calmed down."

"Where were you at the time?" I asked.

"Titusville sector. It's part of Spaceport Administration. We went near it on our way here." He took the shape of an oversized statue of Albert Einstein, and sat in the dust, cross-legged, his eyes at our level. "It was a convenient coincidence, since I would have headed for a spaceport no matter where I'd been at the time. Waiting for someone to come explain what has happened."

"I don't think we know any more than you," Marygay said.

"You know your own circumstances. Maybe together we can come up with something." He looked off to the east. "Your ship is an old-fashioned fighter, Sumi class, and its communication system has safeguards that prevented it from telling me much. I know you came from Middle Finger via the Aleph-10 collapsar. The ship also knows you, and it, were somewhere else before, but it can't say where."

"We were in the middle of nowhere," I said, "a tenth of a light-year from Middle Finger. We'd taken a converted cruiser and were headed out twenty thousand light-years—"

"I remember that from the Tree. I thought the request was denied."

"We sort of hijacked it," Marygay said.

Einstein nodded. "Some people suggested you might. That they should have let you go ahead with it, to prevent violence."

"One of me was killed," said the Tauran.

There was an uncomfortable silence. The Omni said something in Tauran, and Antres replied, "True."

"We'd gone about a tenth of a light-year, when the antimatter fueling the cruiser suddenly evaporated."

"Evaporated? Do you have a *scientific* explanation for that?" Einstein grew a third eye and blinked it.

"No. The ship suggested 'transient-barrier virtual particle substitution,' but as far as I could find out, it doesn't apply. Anyhow, we limped back to Middle Finger in these converted Sumi fighters, and found everybody gone. It turns out that if you make corrections for relativistic simultaneity, they disappeared the same time our antimatter did.

"We assumed that our being off Middle Finger had saved us. But it happened here, too."

He stroked his huge moustache. "Perhaps you caused it."

"What?"

"You just posited the argument yourself. If two improbable things happen simultaneously, they must be related. Maybe one caused the other."

"No. If putting a bunch of people in a starship and accelerating caused impossible things to happen, we would have noticed long ago."

"But you weren't going anywhere. Except the future."

"I don't think the universe cares about our intent."

Einstein laughed. "That's your belief system again. You just used the word 'impossible' to describe events you know did happen."

Cat was amused. "You have to admit he has a point."

"Okay. But the other anomaly is that *you* guys are still here, when all the humans and Taurans disappeared. So maybe *you* caused it."

He changed into a huge Indian brave, I suppose a Timu-cuan, scarred with elaborate tattoos, impressively naked, smelling like a wet goat. "That's more like it. Though I'll ask the others about virtual particle transient barrier, whatever. Some of them know science."

"Can you talk to them now, like telepathy?" Cat asked.

"No, not unless they're in my line of sight. The way I talked to your ship. We used to just call each other up, but most of the systems are failing. We leave messages on the Tree now."

"We ought to check the Tree again ourselves," the sheriff said, "Antres and I."

"Especially the Tauran Tree," the brave said. "We can tap it, but a lot of it is confusing."

"I'm afraid much of it is confusing to me as well," Antres said. "I'm from Tsogot. We're in contact with Earth, or were in contact, but our cultures have been diverging for centuries."

"That might be useful." The brave changed into a kindly-looking old man. "A doubly alien perspective." He produced a blue package of cigarettes and lit one, wrapped in yellow paper, which smelled even more noxious than the one before. I sorted through grandfatherly images and came up with Walt Disney.

"Why are so many of your images from the twentieth century?" I asked. "Are you reading our minds, Marygay and me?"

"No, I can't do that. I just like the period—end of inno-cence, before the Forever War. Everything got kind of compli-cated after that." He took a deep drag on the cigarette and closed his eyes, evidently savoring it. "Then it got too simple, if you ask me. We were all sort of waiting for this Man thing to run its course."

"It survived so long because it worked," the sheriff said mildly.

"Termite colonies work," Disney said. "They don't produce interesting conversation." To Antres: "You Taurans got a lot more done, or at least more interesting things, before you had a group mind. I went to Tsogot once, as a xenosociologist, and studied your history."

"It's academic now," I said; "both Man and Tauran. No group, no group mind."

The sheriff shook his head. "We'll grow back, same as you. Most of the frozen ova and sperm are Man."

"You assume the others are all dead," Disney said, "but all we really know is that they've disappeared."

"They're all in some big nudist colony in the sky," I said.

"We have no evidence one way or the other. Your group is here and so is ours. Omni on the Moon and Mars and in local spaceships all report the disappearance of humans and Taurans, but none of *us* is gone, as far as we can tell."

"Other starships?" Stephen said.

"That's why I was waiting at the Cape. There are twenty-four within one collapsar jump of Stargate. Two should have returned by now. But only unmanned drones have come in, with routine messages."

"Why do you think the Omni were spared?" Marygay said. "Because you're immortal?"

"Oh, we're not immortal, except the way an amoeba is." He smiled at me. "If you had targeted me this morning, rather than the hot dog stand, you would probably have done enough damage to kill me."

"I'm sorry—"

He waved it away. "You thought I was a machine. But no, except for you, the thing seems species-selective. Humans and Taurans disappear; birds and bees and Omni don't."

"And the thing that sets us apart is that we were trying to escape," Cat said.

Disney shrugged. "Suppose for a moment that the universe does care about intent. What you were doing would get its notice."

That was a bit much. "And that would piss off the universe so much that it would destroy ten billion people and Taurans."

Anita moaned softly. "Something . . . something's wrong." She stood erect, her back arching, and her eyes grew round and bulged. Her face swelled. Her coveralls became taut and the seams started to split.

Then she exploded: one horrible wet *smack*, and we were all spattered with blood and tissue; a piece of bone glanced off my cheekbone with stinging force.

I looked at the Omni. He was Disney, covered with blood and gore, and then he flickered, between Disney and an apparition that was mostly fangs and claws—and then he was Uncle Walt again, clean.

Most of us, including me, sat down. Chance and Steve sort of fell down. Where Anita had been standing, there were a pair of boots with two blood-streaked stalks of bone.

"I didn't do this," Disney said.

The sheriff drew his pistol. "I don't believe you." He shot him point-blank in the heart.

thirty

The next few minutes were grotesque. The little robots rolled out to clean up—Mickey and Donald and Minnie chanting admonitory rhymes while they speared and vacuumed up the fragmentary remains of a woman I'd known for half my life. When they went to police up her boots, all that was left that had any individuality, I followed the Omni's example and kicked them away. The sheriff saw what I was doing and helped.

We each picked up a gory boot. "There has to be some way to bury her," he said.

Disney sat up, clutching his chest. "If you'll stop shooting me, I can help." He closed his eyes, his skin chalk grey, and for a moment it looked like he was just going to fall back dead. But he transformed himself, slowly, limb by limb, into a large black working man in overalls, clutching a shovel. He got to his feet with exaggerated stiffness.

"You been around these normal people too long," he said in a gravelly Louis Armstrong bass. "You suppose' to control that temper." He whacked a robot away with the shovel, and pointed with it, toward a stand of palm trees. "Let's take her over there, put her to rest." He addressed the others. "You all get inside and clean up. We take care of this part."

He hefted the shovel and walked toward the palms. As he passed the sheriff, he said, "Don't do that. It hurts."

The sheriff and I followed him, each with our grisly token. It took him about a minute to dig a deep square hole.

We put the boots in the hole and he refilled it and patted the dirt smooth. "Did she have a religion?"

"Orthodox New Catholic," I said.

"I can do that." He absorbed the shovel and became a tall priest in a black cowled robe, with tonsure and heavy cross on a chain swinging from his neck. He said a few words in Latin and made a cross gesture over the grave.

Still the priest, he walked with us back to Molly Malone's, where several people were sitting on porch chairs and a rocker. Stephen was weeping uncontrollably, Marygay and Max holding on to him. He and Anita had had a son together, who died in an accident at nine or ten. They drifted apart after that, but were still friends. Rii brought him a glass of water and a pill.

"Rii," I said, "if that's some sort of trank, I could use one myself." I felt as if *I* was about to explode, out of grief and confusion.

She looked at the vial. "It's mild enough. Anybody want to take a nap?" I think everybody took one, except Antres 906 and the priest. Marygay and I went up to the inn's second floor and found a bed, and collapsed in each other's arms.

forever free

*   *   *

It was almost sundown when I woke up. I got out of bed as quietly as possible and found that Molly Malone's plumbing still worked, even to hot water. Marygay got up while I was washing, and we went downstairs together.

Stephen and Matt were making noise in the dining area. They'd pulled several tables together and set out some plastic dishes and forks, and a pile of food boxes. "Our fearless leader," she said. "You get to open the first box."

I didn't really feel like eating, though I should have been famished. I picked up one that said CHILI in bright red letters, with a picture of Donald Duck holding his throat, fire issuing from his beak. I pulled the top back and it worked, the chili sizzling and filling the room with an agreeable odor.

"Not spoiled," I said, and blew on a forkful. It was bland, meatless. "Seems okay."

The others popped boxes, and soon the place smelled like a cafeteria. Cat and Po came down, followed by Max. We ate the small meals in stunned silence, except for mumbled greetings. Po said grace before he opened his box.

I left mine unfinished. "See what the sunset looks like," I said, and got up from the table. Marygay and Cat came along.

Outside, Antres 906 and the Omni, still looking like a priest, were conversing in croaks and squeaks, standing where Anita had died.

"Discussing who the next will be?" Cat said, glaring at the priest.

He looked up, startled. "What?"

"What caused that," she said, "if it wasn't you?"

"Not me. I could do that to myself, if I wanted to die, but I couldn't do it to someone else."

"Couldn't, or wouldn't?" I said.

"Couldn't. 'Physically impossible,' to put it in words of four syllables. To use your belief system."

"So what happened? People don't just explode!"

He sat down on the edge of the porch and crossed his long legs, lacing his fingers over his knee, looking toward the sunset. "There you go again. People do explode, obviously. One just did."

"And it could have been any of us." Marygay's voice shook. "We could all go like that, one by one."

"We could," the priest said, "including me. But I hope it was just an experiment. A test."

"Someone's testing us?" I was feeling dizzy and trying to control nausea. I sat down carefully on the porch floor.

"Always," the priest said quietly. "You've never felt that?"

"Metaphor," I said.

He made a slow sweeping gesture. "The way all this is metaphor. Taurans understand that better than you do."

"Not this," Antres 906 said. "This is something I cannot contain."

"The nameless." The priest said a Tauran word I didn't know.

Antres touched his throat. "Of course. But the . . . you say 'nameless'? They are not literally real. They are a convenience, a symbol, talking about . . . I do not know how to say it. Truth underneath appearance, fate?"

The priest touched his cross and it became a circle with two legs, a Tauran religious icon. "Symbol, metaphor. The nameless, I think, are more real than we are."

"But you've never seen or touched one," I said. "Just guessing."

"No one ever has. You've never seen a neutrino, but you don't doubt their existence. In spite of 'impossible' characteristics."

"All right. But you can prove neutrinos are there, or *something* is there, because otherwise particle physics wouldn't work out. The universe couldn't exist."

"I could just say, 'I rest my case.' You don't like the idea of the nameless because it smacks of the supernatural."

Fair enough. "Okay. But for the first fifty—or fifteen hundred—years of my life, and for thousands of years preceding me, the universe could be explained without resorting to your mysterious nameless." I turned to Antres. "That's also true of Taurans, isn't it?"

"Very much so, yes. The nameless are real, but only as intellectual constructs."

"Let me ask you an old question," the priest said. "How likely is it that humans and Taurans, evolving independently on planets forty light-years apart, would meet at the same level of technology, and be similar enough psychologically to fight a war?"

"A lot of people have asked that question," I nodded toward Antres, "and a lot of Taurans, I suppose. Some of the people from my future, under my command, belonged to a religious sect that had it all explained. Something like your nameless."

"But you have a better explanation?"

"Sorting. If they had been pre-technological, we wouldn't have interacted. If they'd been thousands of years ahead of us, there would have been no war. Extermination, maybe." Antres made a sound of agreement. "So it's partly coincidence, but not completely."

"It was not at all coincidence. We Omni have been on both planets since before humans and Taurans had language, which we gave you. Or technology, which we controlled.

"We were Archimedes, Galileo, and Newton. In your parents' time, we took control of NASA, to retard human development in space."

"And you masterminded the Forever War."

"I don't think so. I think we just set up the initial conditions. You could have cooperated with one another, if it had been in your natures."

"But first you made sure our natures were warlike," Marygay said.

"That I don't know. That would be far before my time." He shook his head. "Let me explain. We're not born the way you are; nor you, Antres 906. I think there are a fixed number of us, around a hundred, and when one of us dies, a new one comes to be.

"You've seen how I can split into two or several pieces. When it's time for a new Omni—when one of us dies somewhere—I or someone else will split, and half will stay separate, and go off to become a new individual."

"With all the parent's memories and skills?" Rii said.

"I *wish*. You start out a duplicate of your parent, but as the months and years go by, that fades away, replaced by your own experience. I would love to have a hundred fifty thousand years of ancestral memory. But all I have is hearsay, passed on by others of my kind."

"Including this 'nameless' stuff," I said.

"That's true. And at various times in my life, I've wondered whether it might not be a delusion—some sort of fiction that we share. Like a religion: there's no way you or I could prove that the nameless *don't* exist. And if they do, their existence can explain the otherwise inexplicable. Like the coincidence of parallel evolution, Taurans and humans coming together at just the right time. Like random people exploding."

"Which happens all the time," Cat said.

"All sorts of inexplicable things happen. Most of them do get explained. I think sometimes the explainers are wrong. If, in the normal course of things, you came upon the remains of someone who had died the way your friend did, you would have assumed foul play; some kind of bomb or something. Not a whim of the nameless."

The sheriff gave words to my thoughts: "I still haven't ruled out foul play. We've watched you do all sorts of things we would call impossible. It is much easier for me to assume you did this, somehow, than to posit the existence of invisible malevolent gods."

"Then why did I do it to her, rather than you? Why didn't I do it to Mandella when he came within an inch of killing me?"

"Maybe you crave excitement," I said. "I've met people like that. You want the two of us to live, to make your world more interesting."

"It's interesting enough, thank you." He cocked his head. "And about to become more so."

book six

THE BOOK OF
REVELATION

I heard it then, the faint warbling sound of two floaters con-
verging from different directions. In a few seconds they were
visible; in a few more, they floated over us and settled down in
the park.

They were sport floaters, bright orange and cherry, stream-
lined like the combat helicopters of my youth—"Cobras," and
they did look like cobras.

The cockpit canopies slid back and a man and a woman
climbed out. They were both a little too large, like our pal, and
the floaters rocked in gratitude, relieved of their weight.

Both the man and the woman shrank when they saw us. But
they left deep footprints in the grass. I wondered why they hadn't
just *come* as floaters. Maybe that took too much material.

The woman was black and stocky, and the man was white
and so plain it would be hard to describe his face. Protective

coloration, I supposed; a kind of default configuration. They were both wearing togas of natural unbleached cloth.

There was no greeting. The three Omni looked at each other, conversing silently, for less than a minute.

The woman spoke. "There will be more of us here soon. We are dying too, in violence, the way your friend died."

"The nameless?" I asked.

"What can you say about the nameless?" the man said. "I think it *is* them, because things are happening contrary to physical law."

"They're in control of *physics*?"

"Apparently," our priest said. "People exploding, antimatter evaporating. Ten billion creatures going off to, as you say, some cosmic nudist colony. Or mass grave."

"I'm afraid it is a grave," the woman said. "And we're about to join them."

All three of them looked at me. The faceless man spoke. "You did it. You tried to leave the Galaxy. Escape the preserve the nameless established for us."

"That's ridiculous," I said. "I've left the Galaxy before. The Sade-138 campaign was in the Greater Magellanic Cloud. Other campaigns were in the Lesser Cloud and the Sagittarius Dwarf."

"Collapsar travel is not the same," the woman said. "Wormholes. It's like exchanging one quantum state for another, and then going back."

"Like a bungee jump," our fan of the twentieth century added.

"With your starship," she continued, "you were actually leaving. You were going into the territory of the nameless."

"They told you this?" Marygay asked. "You talk to the nameless?"

"No," the man said. "It's just inference."

"You would call it Occam's Razor," the woman said. "It's the least complicated explanation."

"So we've provoked the wrath of God," I said.

"If you want to put it that way," the plain one said. "What we're trying to figure out is how to get God's attention."

I wanted to scream, but Sara expressed it more calmly. "If they're omnipotent and everywhere . . . we *have* their attention. Too much of it."

The priest shook his head. "No. It's sporadic. The nameless leave us alone for weeks, for years. Then they introduce a variable, like a scientist or a curious child would, and watch how we react."

"Getting rid of everybody?" Marygay said. "That's a *variable?*"

"No," the black woman said. "I think it means the experiment is over. The nameless are cleaning up."

"And what we have to do," the plain man said, and paused. "Now me." He exploded, but not into blood and guts and fragments of bone. It was a shower of white particles, a small blizzard. The particles settled to the ground and disappeared.

"Hell," the priest said. "I liked him."

"What we have to do," the woman continued for him, "is get the attention of the nameless and convince them to leave us alone."

"And you two," the priest said to me and Marygay, "are the obvious key. You provoked them."

Max had disappeared. He came back inside the fighting suit. "Max," I said, "be real. We can't fight them that way."

"We don't know," he said softly. "We don't know anything."

"We still don't know if you're telling the truth," Sara said. "The nameless stuff might be so much sand. *You* did it—you killed everybody off and now you're playing with us. You can't prove otherwise, can you?"

"One of us just died," the priest said.

"No, he changed state and disappeared," I said.

The priest smiled. "Exactly. Isn't that what you do when you die?"

"Drop it," Marygay said. "If it is the Omni, and an elaborate ghastly joke, we're doomed no matter what we do. So we might as well take them at face value." Sara opened her mouth to say something and closed it.

"Oh, shit," Max said, and the fighting suit rocked and stood rigid.

"Again," the priest said.

"Max!" I shouted. "Are you there?" Nothing.

Marygay moved behind the suit, where the emergency release was. "Should I do this?"

"Have to, sooner or later," I said. "Sara . . ."

"I can take it. I saw Anita," she said, her pale face going to chalk.

Marygay popped the suit, and it was about as bad as I had imagined. There was nothing you could identify as Max. Gallons of blood and other fluids sloshed out on the ground. Chunks of muscle and organs and bone filled the lower part of the suit.

Sara crouched and vomited. I almost did the same, but an old combat reflex made me clench my teeth and swallow, hard, three times.

Max was the kind of guy you liked in spite of what he did; in spite of who he was. And they just took him out like removing a piece from a game.

"Can we be part of this?" I yelled. "Is there any way we can make a case for ourselves?"

Cat exploded like a bomb. Not even organs and bones, this time; just a fine mist blowing away from where she had been standing. Marygay moaned and fainted. Sara, I think, didn't even notice. She was on her knees, sobbing, her arms wrapped around herself while her body spasmed, trying to empty an empty stomach.

There were two explosions inside Molly Malone's, and hysterical screaming.

Antres 906 looked at me. "I am ready," he said in slow English. "I do not want to be here anymore. Let the nameless take me."

I nodded numbly and went to Marygay. Kneeled and lifted her head and tried with a tissue to wipe her face clean, clean of what remained of the woman she loved. She half woke, her eyes still closed, and put an arm around my waist. She rocked silently, breathing hard.

It was a closeness not many people could have, the way we'd felt sometimes in battle, or just before: We're going to die now, but we're going to die together.

"Forget the nameless," I said. "We've been on borrowed time since the day we were drafted . . . and we've—"

"Stolen time," she said, her eyes still closed. "And we made a good life out of it."

"I love you," we said at the same time.

There was a loud *thump;* the fighting suit had fallen over. The breeze reversed itself and became a wind, blowing toward the suit. Something stung the back of my neck—a bone or a piece of one, again—and it tumbled on into the suit.

With a sound like dry sticks rattling, an incomplete skeleton heaved itself upright from the open casket of the suit. A forearm, ulna and radius, attached itself to the right elbow; metacarpals grew out of the wrist, and fingerbones grew out of the meta-carpals.

Then a long coil of blue intestines settled onto the pelvic girdle, and a stomach on top, a bladder, faster and faster; liver, lungs, heart, nerves, and muscles. The skull fell forward with the weight of a brain, and it rose slowly to look at me with Max's blue eyes. For a moment, the face was red and white, like a flayed specimen. But then skin appeared, and hair; and then skin and hair all over the body.

He stepped out of the suit, gingerly, and clothing grew on him, a loose white robe. He walked toward us with a fixed, intense expression. He, or it.

Marygay was sitting up now. "What's happening?" she said, in a voice so tight it cracked.

It sat down cross-legged in front of us. "You're a scientist."

"Max?"

"I don't have a name. You're a scientist."

"You're the nameless?"

He waved that away. "William Mandella. You *are* a scientist."

"Trained as one. Science teacher, now."

"But you understand the nature of research. You understand what an experiment is."

"Of course."

The Omni had come over to join us. He nodded toward the black woman. "Then she was pretty close to the truth."

"The experiment's over?" she said. "And you're cleaning up?"

He shook his head slowly. "How can I put it? First the mice you're examining escape the cage. Then they understand what's happening to them. Then they demand to talk to the experimenter."

"If it were me," I said, "I'd talk to the mice."

"Yes, that's what a human would do." He looked around, with a vaguely annoyed expression.

"So talk," Marygay said.

He looked at her for a long moment. "When you were a little girl, you wet the bed. Your parents wouldn't let you go to camp until you stopped."

"I'd forgotten that."

"I don't forget." He turned to me. "Why don't you like lima beans?"

I drew a blank. "We don't have lima beans on Middle Finger. I don't even remember what they taste like."

"When you were three Earth years old, you stuck a dry lima bean up your nose. Trying to get it out, you pushed it farther up. Your mother finally figured out what you were crying about, and her ministrations made it worse. It began to swell, with the moisture. She took you to the commune's holistic healer, and *he* made it worse still. By the time they got you to a hospital, they had to put you to sleep to extract it, and you had sinus problems for some time."

"You did that?"

"I watched it. I set up the initial conditions, a long time before you were born, so, in a way, yes, I did. Every sparrow that falls, I hear the thump, and the thump never surprises me."

"Sparrows?"

"Never mind." He made a small dismissive shrug. "The experiment's over. I'm leaving."

"Leaving?"

He stood up. "This galaxy." There was an explosion of soil, and the feet we'd buried flew back to where Anita had been standing when she died. Bits of flesh and bone and a mist of red sucked through the air toward the ghastly remnants, and began to reconstruct her. Ten feet away, Cat's body was reassembling itself from the air.

"I don't guess I need to straighten up," he said; it said. "I'll just leave you on your own. Check back in a million years or so."

"Just us?" Marygay said. "You killed ten billion people and Taurans, and now you're handing five empty planets over to us?"

"Six," it said, "and they're not empty. The people and Taurans aren't dead. Just put away."

"Put *away*?" I said. "Where did you put them?"

It smiled at me like someone holding back a punch line. "How much space, how much volume, do you think it takes to store ten billion people?"

"God, I don't know. A big island?"

"One and a third cubic miles. They're all stacked in Carlsbad Caverns. And now they're awake, and cold and naked and hungry." It looked at its watch. "Guess I could leave them some food."

"Middle Finger?" I said. "They're alive, too?"

"In a grain elevator in Vendler," it said. "They're *really* cold. I'll do something for them. Have done."

"You do things faster than the speed of light?"

"Sure. That's just one of the constraints I put on the experiment." It scratched its chin. "Think I'll leave it. Otherwise you'd be all over the place."

"The Moon and Mars? Heaven and Kysos?"

It nodded. "Mostly cold and hungry. Hot and hungry on Heaven. But they'll all probably find some food before they're reduced to eating one another."

It looked at Marygay and me. "You two are special, since nobody else remembers as far back as you do. It amused me to construct your situation.

"But to me, time is like a table, or a floor. I can walk back to the Big Bang, or forward to the heat death of the universe. Life and death are reversible conditions. Trivial ones, to me. As you have seen here."

I shouldn't have said it, but I did. "So now it amuses you to let us live?"

"That's one way to put it. Or you could say I'm leaving the experiment to cook on its own. I'll walk forward a million years and see what happens."

"But you already know the future," Marygay said.

The thing inside Max rolled his eyes. "It isn't a *line*. It's a table. There are all kinds of futures. Else why bother to experiment?"

Sara spoke up. "Don't leave!" He looked at her with an impatient expression. "We see things like a line, a line of cause and effect. But you see millions of lines on your table."

"An infinity of lines."

"Okay. Is there anything else in the universe besides your table?" He smiled. "Are there other tables? Is there a room?"

"There are other tables. If they're in a room, I've never seen the walls."

Then it spoke in exact unison with Sara: "So is there someone else in charge?" By herself: "In charge of all of you and your tables?"

"Sara," it said, "in some of those many lines, you choose to be alive a million years from now, when I return. You may ask me then. Or you may not need to."

"But if there isn't anyone else; if you're God—"

"What?" Max said. He rubbed the white cloth between his fingers. "What the hell is going on here?" He looked over at the fighting suit. "I felt this horrible pain, all over."

"Me, too," Cat said. She was sitting cross-legged on the spot where she had died, one hand in her lap and the other over her breasts. "And then I was suddenly here, back again. But you got clothes." She looked at us with raised eyebrows. "What the hell is going on?"

"God knows," I said.

thirty-two

I worried for a few seconds about what to do with ten billion people and Taurans stranded naked in the middle of the desert. But the nameless had waved its wand one last time.

The air around us shimmered, and we were suddenly surrounded by a thick crowd of men, women, and children, all naked, many screaming.

A small cluster of people with clothes on does stand out in that situation. People began to approach us tentatively, and Marygay and I both braced for leadership.

Of course it didn't happen. An older Man walked straight up to me and started asking loud, pointed questions.

But I couldn't understand a word of it. I spoke a dead language that, on this planet, I shared with only a handful of scholars and immigration people.

The three Omni stepped up, tall enough to draw attention,

arms up and shouting something in unison. The priest touched my shoulder. "We'll see what we can do here. You help your own people."

Marygay was standing with a protective arm around Cat. I took off my shirt and gave it to her; it was just big enough to cover the essentials.

In fact, it looked kind of sexy. A popular woman once told me that the way to attract attention at a party was to wear a long dress when you knew the others would be in jeans or shorts, and vice versa. So if you're at a party where everyone is naked, any old thing will do.

We finally herded everyone together in Molly Malone's. The cafeteria was jammed with hungry people, so we gathered in the "Social History of Prostitution" room, or however it translates. The exhibits were unambiguous.

Seven of us had been killed and reconstructed. We tried to explain to them what had happened. As if we could actually understand.

God killed a bunch of you, to get our attention. Then He announced He was leaving, and revived you and ten billion others on His way out.

I kept waiting to wake up. Like the old guy in *A Christmas Carol,* I was thinking this had to be something I ate.

As it went on and on, of course, that possibility faded. Maybe everything *before* had been a dream.

The sheriff and Antres 906 got in touch with their Trees and let everybody know what apparently had happened. The Omni amiably revealed their existence and helped pull things together. There was a little more involved than just finding clothes for everybody.

Finding a "place" for everybody was going to take a while: one thing human, Man, and Tauran cultures had in common was the assumption of the immutability of physical law. We may not understand everything, but everything does follow rules, which are eventually knowable.

That was gone now. We had no idea what parts of physics had been a whim of the nameless. It had laid claim to the constancy and limitation of the speed of light, which meant that most of post–Newtonian physics was part of the joke.

It had said it was going to leave that unaffected, to keep us in our cage. Were there other laws, assumptions, constants that did not please it? All of science was in question now, and had to be checked.

Religion was less in question, interestingly enough. Just change a few terms, and ignore uncertainty as to the existence of God. God's intent had never been that clear, anyhow. The nameless had left the faithful incontrovertible proof of its existence, and enough new data for millenniums of fruitful theological debate.

My own religion, if you can call it that, had changed in its fundamental premise, but not its basic assertion: I'd always told religious friends that there may or may not be a God, but if there is one, I wouldn't want to have him over for dinner. I'll stand by that last part.

thirty-three

After a couple of weeks, there was little we could do or learn on Earth, and we were anxious to get back. The Omni who had met us at our arrival wanted to go along, and I was glad to include it. A few magic tricks would make our fantastic story more acceptable.

Nobody died on the jump, so five months later we came out of the SA coffins and stared down at Middle Finger, blinding white with snow and cloud. We should have found a few years of stuff to do on Earth; come back in thaw or spring.

There was no one on duty at the spaceport, but we were able to get through to the Office for Interplanetary Communications, and they had a flight controller sent out. It took us a couple of hours to transfer to the shuttle, anyhow.

The landing was a big improvement over our last one: reassuring lines of smoke from chimneys in outlying towns; a snarl of winter traffic in Centrus.

A woman who identified herself as mayor came out in the transfer vehicle, along with her Man liaison—and Bill, who got the most attention from Marygay and Sara and me. He was growing a beard, but otherwise hadn't changed much.

Except perhaps in his attitude toward me. He wept when we embraced, as I did, and for a minute couldn't do anything but shake his head. Then in heavily accented English he said, "I thought I'd lost you forever, you stubborn old bastard."

"Sure, *me* stubborn," I said. "Good to have you back. Even though you're city folk now."

"Actually, we're back in Paxton"—he blushed—"my wife Auralyn and I. We went back to set the place up. Plenty of fish. Figured you'd come back soon, if you were coming back, so I came into Centrus last week to wait.

"Charlie's with me in town. Diana's stuck in Paxton, doctoring. What the hell happened?"

I groped for words. "It's kind of complicated." Marygay was trying not to laugh. "You'll be glad to know I found God."

"*What?* On Earth?"

"But he just said hello-goodbye and left. It's a long story." I looked out at the snow, plowed higher than the vehicle's windows. "Plenty of time to talk, before things get busy in the thaw."

"Eight cords of wood," he said. "Ten more on the way."

"Good." I tried to summon up the warm memory of sitting around the fireplace, but reality intruded. Slipping around on the ice, pulling in fish that froze in the air. Plumbing jammed by frozen pipes. And shovel, shovel, shovel snow.

thirty-four

We resumed "everyday" life in the sense of fishing and fighting the winter, though we were suddenly a household of five adults. Sara still had a term of school left before she could start university, but she got permission to wait a few months rather than start at midterm and play catch-up.

Life in Paxton had resumed pretty much unchanged, once people found their way back from Centrus. We lived with constant power outages during the winter in the best of times, so it wasn't hard to cope with a semi-permanent one.

The town had been almost completely repopulated in a few weeks. Centrus had put a high priority on getting rid of anybody who could leave, since the city's resources were strained to the limit, providing essentials for the people who normally lived there.

The capital was settling down after five months of chaos.

Eight winters' exposure had left the city a shambles, but it was obvious that most repairs would have to wait till thaw and spring. Our group of involuntary pioneers had helped the city organize itself on a temporary bare-survival footing. The lack of a central power system would have been the death of all of the city dwellers, if anybody had been simple-minded enough just to go home. Instead, people packed together in large public shelters, to conserve heat and simplify the distribution of food and water.

I'm sure it was all very chummy, but I was just as happy to be out in the provinces, with our cords of wood and boxes of candles. The university was open in the daytime, though most normal instruction was postponed, waiting for the power grid to give us back our computers and viewscreens, and most of all our library. We did have a couple of thousand printed books, but they were a disorganized collection of this and that.

One of them, fortunately, was a thick text about theoretical mechanics, so I could start on what was going to be my life's work. I'd discussed it with some Man physicists on Earth: all of us had to go back to Square One and find out how much of physics was still intact. If the whole thing was just a set of constraints that the nameless had set up, and changed at whim, then it behooved us to find out what the current state of whims was! And it seemed like a good idea to do the experiments on other planets, as well as Earth, to see whether the laws were uniform.

Bill joined me in the laboratories that winter, acting as my assistant while we reproduced the basic experiments of eighteenth- and nineteenth-century physics. Weights and springs. We did have the advantage of accurate atomic clocks, or so we thought. Within a year we'd find out, from Earth, that the nameless had left us a truly Sisyphean job: the speed of light was still finite, but it had changed by about 5 percent. That screwed up everything, down around the fourth decimal place. Little things like the charge on the electron, Planck's constant. While he was at it, he should have made pi equal to three.

But things were all right with us, waiting out the cold in our warm lab, rolling balls down inclines, measuring pendulums, stretching springs, then going home to the women. Bill had met Auralyn when they'd both volunteered to become Man, and they fell in love before any damage had been done, and came back here. She was going to have a baby in the spring.

Meanwhile, we chip ice, shovel snow, thaw pipes, scrape windows. Winter lasts forever on this god-forsaken world.